DEADLY MISTAKE

- a novel

DEADLY MISTAKE

- a novel

Ty Michael

Copyright © 2020 Ty Michael
Revised, 2021

All rights reserved.

This is a work of fiction. Names, characters, businesses, places, events, locales, and incidents are either the products of the author's imagination or used in a fictitious manner. Any resemblance to actual persons, living or dead, or actual events is purely coincidental.

No part of this publication may be reproduced, or transmitted by any means, electronic, digital, mechanical, photocopying, or otherwise without written permission from the publisher.

[July, 2019] - [Jan, 2020]

chapter one

The taste of blood was the first thing I noticed after the crash. Everything hurt … it hurt so bad. When the car began flipping down the mountain after going off of the road, I tried my best to cover my head and squeeze my elbows against my face.

All was quiet now except for the low hissing sound coming from under the buckled hood.

I could feel a cool breeze blowing on my face through where the windshield used to be.

My eyes opened slowly and I unclasped my hands from the back of my head. I let out a shallow breath and carefully licked my bottom lip only to feel a burn and something hard stuck to it. Glass. A sharp puff of air sent the glass shard into the now-deflated white air bag along with a splatter of red.

Pain everywhere. Pain along with the tingling sensation of the blood dripping across the fresh cuts on my arms and neck. A throbbing from my left leg took hold as the adrenaline faded away.

My mind flooded with fleeting snapshots.

I remember driving. I remember the left curve. Two-lane road. The truck. Yes, the white truck. It passed me on the inside as we were taking the left curve. It clipped the front of my car when it moved over in front of me.

Then I slammed the brakes. But it was too late. I felt the passenger front tire go over first. The steering wheel jerked. My foot to the floor on the brake and my hands tried like hell to turn the car back onto the road. The loose gravel. The car wouldn't stop. Like slow motion, the world seemed to turn sideways as the car left the road. Letting go of the steering wheel when I saw only dirt and rocks through the windshield, I covered up the best I could. I remember feeling upside down on the first flip. After that, it was just a tumble over and over again with hard jolts as the car crashed into things on its way down. Maybe trees. Maybe rocks. The car finally came to a hard, sudden stop at the bottom. Upright. Luckily, I guess.

My leg. Looking down at it, I didn't see blood. That was good. I could move my foot. That was good. Bending my knee was doable. It throbbed like hell, but wasn't broken. Just banged up. Must have gotten jammed against the door or lower dash in the rolling. I glanced up toward the sky from where the driver's side window once was and could see the edge of the road about two hundred feet up. Almost straight up. Reaching down and rubbing my knee, I said aloud to myself, "Making it up to the road is going to be tough. But I'm alive."

I need to let Daniel know, I thought. By habit, I felt for my cell phone in the dash console where I'd always kept it when I drove. Not there. *Crap, it could be anywhere on this piece of mountain.* I looked all around. It hurt to twist my head and neck. I winced as I pushed myself up in the seat to peer over into the back floorboard. Something was holding me down. Something. My mind still wasn't right. The seatbelt. The seatbelt that most likely saved my life was still doing its job despite the rest of the car having given up. I unbuckled it, pushed myself up and saw my phone on the floorboard mixed in among the glass pieces and spruce tree needles.

Stretching my right arm as far as I could, with fingertips extending their most, I felt the corner of the phone and managed to scoot it close enough for me to grab.

With a sigh, I settled back into my seat and activated the phone. While thinking of how to say things, my eyes scanned over my white blouse and black dress slacks. I shook my head, noticing the blood, glass, and orange mountain dust covering them.

The service was almost non-existent. I went to the 'My Favorites' section and tapped Daniel's cell number. Ringing … ringing … ringing … voice mail. "Hi, you've reached Daniel Cline. Leave a message and I'll return your call. *Beep.*"

"Daniel, I've been in a wreck. I'm hurt, but I don't think too bad. I love you. Tell the girls I love them. I'll be ok. I need to go now and call for help. I love you. I love you."

chapter two

The soccer game was a heated one. One more goal and the girls' team would win. After an entire season, this win would be their first. Daniel stood on the sidelines watching Olivia and Mattie's team. They had the ball. Mattie was faster, but Olivia was deadly accurate. For twins, they only looked similar. Everything else about them was so different. At ten years old, they were a year younger than the other soccer girls, but just as good. At least Daniel thought so.

Daniel's phone vibrated in the front pocket of his jeans.

Mattie intercepted a pass from the other team. She quickly switched feet and direction and headed to the goal. The sea of ponytails and yellow and blue uniforms all turned at the same time like a flock of birds in the sky. Mattie passed the ball to a teammate to the right then veered off left to dodge two blue uniforms that slowed trying to follow the ball change. Olivia jogged near the goal, watching the ball. Waiting for a pass. She was open. She was ready. The ball flew to her across a fifty foot patch of green. Her eyes on it. In an instant, a blue uniform closed the gap and hit the soccer ball with the leading edge of her foot, but it was a bad hit and in the effort to reclaim the ball, it skimmed past the white line. The sound of the whistle seemed to match the look on Olivia's face. So close.

Remembering that missed phone call, Daniel pulled his phone out and saw Kaitlyn's name on the missed call screen. Just below the missed call alert read *one new voice mail*. Walking away from the field, he touched the button and put the phone to his ear.

Immediately, he could tell the message may not be audible due to bad service on her end. "Dan ..., I've been ... a wreck." The message went in and out and he tried to put the mumbled sounds together in his head. He could only make out, "I'm hurt, but ... bad. I love you. Tell ... girls I love them. I'll be ... I need to go now ... I love you. I love you." The sound trailed off to silence.

Daniel repeated the message again, listening intently.

He dialed her back. The worst of thoughts going through his mind. It went right to voice mail, "Hi, this is Kaitlyn, I can't answer right now. Leave a message. *Beep.*"

Daniel spoke loudly into his phone, "Baby, let me know if you are ok. I'm gonna call 911. Let me know where you are. Please, baby ... be ok. Please, please."

His thumbs hurriedly dialed 911 and the dispatcher picked up quick. "911. What is your emergency?"

"My wife." Daniel answered, "my wife got in a wreck. A car wreck. She called me, but I missed it. She left a message. She won't answer now." Daniel spoke fast, but the dispatcher understood his frantic sentences from her experience with similar calls.

She asked, "Do you have a location?"

"No, I don't. I'm here in North Carolina and she's in Colorado," Daniel replied, rubbing his head spastically with his fingers running through his hair. "Shit, I don't know."

The dispatcher asked, "Do you know the last city she was in?"

"Yes," he nearly shouted, "Aspen. She stayed in Aspen last night."

"Do you know where she was going next?"

"Something Vista … she was going to Buena Vista." He slapped the palm of his hand against his forehead. "But I don't know the road. I don't know how she was going."

"It's ok," she said. "Stay on the line with me for a few more questions and then I'll contact the Aspen Police Department and let them know. They will know where to search for her."

"Ok."

"What's her name, physical description, and what make, model, and color of car was she in?"

Daniel was walking in fast circles in the grass without even knowing he was doing it. "Kaitlyn. Kaitlyn Cline. Kaitlyn F. Cline. She's my wife. She's five-six, athletic build, with long light brown hair. The car is a rental. She rented it after she landed in Denver. I don't know the kind of car. Or the color."

chapter three

After leaving Daniel the message, I laid my head back in the seat. I knew that I needed to get up to the road and flag someone down. I could call 911, but I had no idea of exactly where I was. And they'd never find me down here. I bent my left knee and my eyes automatically closed and my teeth clamped down tight at the sharp jab of pain. The cuts on my arms stung and little rivers of dried blood covered my bare skin.

    First, it was the sound of one lone tiny rock hitting the metal near the front of the car that got my attention. I looked up to the road above and saw them. Two men. Ordinary-looking men. One was standing at the road's edge and the other had begun to sidestep down the steep incline toward me. Rocks and dust were coming loose at each careful and steady step. A skinny guy with slicked-back dark hair. More small rocks began to fall, bouncing down and hitting the car, flying through the interior. He shouted, "Hey, you in there!"

"Yes," I replied as loud as possible. I could talk, but shouting just wasn't going to happen. When I attempted, my chest hurt. My gut hurt. I wrapped my right arm around my midsection, more for mental comfort than anything else.

He repeated, "Are you in there?"

He must not have been able to see me inside due to the bright sunlight reflecting off the crumpled metal. I leaned to the side window and gave a wave of my hand. Settling back in my seat, I let out a breath of relief. They'd flag a car down. They'd get help. I closed my eyes and waited.

"*Pop!* ... *Pop, pop!*" Along with those *pops* were two loud *ting* sounds that hit the driver's side door. I tensed, turned my head up to him, and I saw it. The pistol. From this distance, it was only a small black object clasped between his hands. But I knew what it was.

The man coming down the incline braced himself against a rock still more than a hundred feet away. He pointed the pistol at the car. At me. "*Pop!* ... *Pop!*"

My mind went blank. I let the phone fall from my hand and I threw my upper body over the center console and armrest into the passenger seat as best and as fast as I could. The shooting stopped. It was over. He thinks he got me. *Stay still Kaitlyn*, I thought to myself. While lying across the front two seats of the car, covering my head, I noticed my purse on the front passenger floorboard. Slowly, I slipped my left hand inside the front pocket and felt for my little coin wallet. Credit cards, ID, some cash. It held the basics.

I heard a distant shout, "Hey, did you get her?" The voice must have been from the guy on the road.

An answer, "I think so. I don't know."

"You better make sure."

"Awe come on, man. You want me to climb all the way down there?" the nearest voice asked.

"You better."

"Shit," the nearest voice fussed.

"Shit," I muttered to myself, copying his sentiment. Carefully sliding the small wallet into my front pants pocket, I began to work my legs into a ball, bringing all of me into the passenger seat of the car. My rear on the center console and my shoulder pushed up against the passenger door that was also missing its window.

Rocks resumed falling and bouncing onto the car, some of them making their way into the cab, hitting me. Through the corner of the driver's side support pillar, I could see him taking careful steps as he descended down the mountainside. He was moving slow, but he was moving and I wasn't. He sounded so much closer than he was. The falling dust and rocks were only making this outcome even more imminent.

I lifted my head and noticed a batch of trees only fifteen feet past the passenger door. I truly didn't know if I could run. I doubted it. Reaching up, I tested the door handle. Nothing. It wouldn't budge. I could still hear him working his way down to me.

"Hurry up," the guy from the road yelled.

I tucked my legs up under my ass as much as possible with the toes of my shoes pressed into the plastic of the console. Bracing my hands against the passenger seat, I got ready. I didn't have time to wait or think. In as quick a motion as I could, I pushed off with my legs and guided my body through the broken passenger window and let myself fall onto the dirt and rocks just on the outside of the car. "*Pop, pop, pop, … pop.*" In a hurry, I regained composure and scrambled to push my back up against the passenger door and gather my legs in close to me. Wrapping my arms around my knees in order to make myself as small and compact as possible, I listened.

"You get her this time?" the man on the road asked loudly.

"Workin' on it." The shooter sounded like he'd stopped moving. Possibly re-bracing himself on the hill. Waiting. Waiting to finish the job. Waiting to finish me. I felt a burn on my shoulder. Fresh blood. Torn blouse. Something cut me when I pushed through the window's opening. Glass or twisted metal.

The batch of trees was barely beyond the car. Only fifteen feet away. If I could get to those trees, I'd have at least a hundred feet of thin forest to go through to gain distance. And get away. Hopefully.

The guy from the road shouted down, "Hold on, there's a car coming."

I turned my head toward the hill and stretched my neck. Probably the dumbest thing to do, but I had to see how close he was. About seventy-five feet away and still quite a distance up the hill. He had his lower foot on the base of a tiny tree growing out of the hill and the other anchored in the loose rocks.

He was looking right at me. The pistol in his right hand and his left was holding onto some sort of tree root. He didn't lift the pistol. He only stared at me as he waited for the all clear from above.

I missed my opportunity.

I heard the *hum* of a car as it passed on the road above and completed the left curve that I never had a chance to.

"Ok, you're good now," the man up top shouted.

I sat back down on my butt and backed up against the metal car door again, out of direct sight.

The trees.

I could make it.

He was still over seventy feet away and those trees were only fifteen. I could make it.

Rocks and dust began to tumble down the hill again, letting me know he was coming.

I lifted my butt and pulled my legs up under me into a squat. The palms of my hands were against the cool metal door, ready to push off.

I only waited a couple seconds, but it felt like forever. I waited until I heard him take another step on the loose, uneven terrain.

I took a breath and ... went for it.

I exerted as much energy as I could in that first burst. My right leg was all adrenaline, but my left leg folded. The knee buckled and I fell forward into the dirt only five feet away from the safety of the car. I was in the open.

My legs tensed and I pulled them up under me again, ready for another burst. I didn't look back, only forward to the trees. I pushed hard with my right leg as I started to scramble. Thrusting forward in spurts with one leg, using my hands to keep balance. My left leg dragged behind, serving only as stability to stop me from face-planting into the dirt again.

I reached the first single tree without hearing another gunshot. Keeping up my hustle, I didn't slow.

Almost there.

"*Pop.*" One single shot. I heard the sound before I ... felt the impact.

Like a hammer hitting me in the lower back. The shot. The impact flattened me. Everything gave out and my body collapsed in the dirt under the spruce trees.

My face in the dirt and spruce tree needles. I closed my eyes. My fingers dug into the loose dirt, instinctively trying to gain traction and continue my escape. My legs motionless. Numb. No pain, no tingling. Like they weren't there anymore.

Sounds began to fade away. A cold sensation came over my body.

I drifted.

My mind drifted. As if going to sleep.

The voice. The sound of a voice in a tunnel. "I got her!" it shouted.

chapter four

The old man sat upright on a white leather couch looking out of the window to the ocean beyond the deck. Between his thumb and index finger, he rolled a large cigar back and forth with steady repetition. He was alone on the couch with one leg crossed over the other, looking out at the tanned bodies lying on the sand and kids running around just in front of the blue-green expanse of water. Thick, brushed-back platinum-silver hair. Gold-rimmed sunglasses. A white suit that matched the couch, and brown patent leather shoes. His cell phone on the couch next to him.

When the phone vibrated and rang, he looked down at the number and let it continue for two more rings. Leaning forward, the old man set his cigar on the ashtray before picking up the phone.

"The job done?" he asked in a thick Cuban accent as soon as he put the phone to his ear. He listened to the answer, then asked to be sure, "And this, you are positive of? Did you check her?"

He stood up with the phone and paced to the window. "But you did not go make sure? So what. I don't care about a fucking mountain. Walk your lazy ass down there. You should have made sure. Go back."

The old man, still at the window, leaned forward and placed his forehead against the large glass pane and looked down at the floor while he heard the caller's argument. When the caller finished, the old man said, "Go back. If there are police or whatever there, then leave. Simple. If no one is at the scene, go check her." He thumped his forehead against the glass. "You do a job, you do it right. You are of no use to me if you can't."

chapter five

My eyes blinked open and my body felt as if it weighed a thousand pounds. I remembered once as a kid, I was at a slumber party and I tried to hide between a mattress and a box spring. When the other girls saw me, they all laid on top of the mattress. I felt like that, like I was being held down. The throbbing pain in my back was unlike anything I'd ever felt.

I could feel my legs, though. Lying in the mountain dirt, I commanded my toes to wiggle inside my shoes. But even that sent jolts of pain to my back. I had to move. I had to. Lifting my face out of the dirt, I carefully turned to look up the mountain. They were gone and I had no idea of how much time had elapsed.

My right hand reached down and lightly touched my lower back. I felt the wetness. Bringing my hand back up in front of my face, I saw red. The palm of my hand was covered in half-dried blood. My side was killing me as well, somewhere around the right hip. Still flat on the dirt, I forced myself to draw up my right leg some in order to shift my body sideways slightly. As soon as I began to bend the knee, my nerves spasmed and I flattened back out on the ground. I reached down again with my hand, to my hip this time, just above the belt. More wetness. More blood.

Pushing hard and gritting my teeth, I managed to tilt myself sideways only a little, supported by my right knee. Contorting my body, I attempted to find some position that was void of the pain, if only for a brief moment. The tiny movement sent my heart racing. My heavy breathing was similar to being winded from a long run. I held the position, letting my body relax. Relax as much as possible.

I spit in the dirt. A dry, foamy wad of spit. It hurt to do it, but I needed to see. I needed to see if it was bloody.

No. No blood. On that positive note, I made my right knee bend more and managed to plant my shoe against a rock. Against the rock, I pressed hard with a steady motion. The pain was immense, but I was able to push myself forward about an inch through the dust and needles.

I rested.

I needed to get help. I needed to get out of here before dark. And I needed to figure out who was trying to kill me?

I gave another push and gained another inch or two. A little less pain.

Another push.

Another couple of inches. A spruce tree with low hanging branches was only a foot away.

Another push.

Reaching the tree, I was able to get a grip on one branch. I grabbed hold of it close to the trunk, where it had some substance. Still on my left side, I used the tight grip on the branch to tug and roll myself over to my belly. Now facedown at the base of the tree, holding onto the branch white-knuckled, I slowly and painfully started to drag my knees up under me. It was a tedious process, one knee at a time, bit by bit.

I rested.

I heaved in and out deeply due to the pain, the fear, and the altitude.

After many minutes of struggle, my body was finally upright and resting on both knees at the base of the tree. A heavy coating of orange dirt was plastered onto my blouse and pants. Dragging myself across the ground had worked each tiny particle of mountain soil deep into the fabric.

I rested there with my eyes closed and attempted to use mind over matter to dull the pain. I knew the next step was to get one foot under me for the task of pushing up into a standing position. I steadied my breathing. In … out … in … out. I forced myself to breathe as I did when I had the twins. Steady and thought-out breaths in preparation for the pain.

I decided to try my left leg for the push up. The knee still hurt, but nothing compared to my right hip. With my eyes closed, I grasped that branch even more tightly and shifted my body weight, lifting the left knee up. A sharp stab of pain made me stop and I almost fell over, catching myself against the ground with my left hand. The movement had placed all of my weight onto the right hip, but I had a foot under me and that was progress. "Come on, Kaitlyn," I told myself. "Come on." Twisting my foot side to side, I anchored the sole of my left shoe into the ground firmly. I couldn't have the shoe slide on my attempt to rise.

In one quick motion, I pulled on the branch, pushed off with my left hand, and shifted all of my weight onto my left leg. All very weak movements, but the combination of them in unison brought me to a stand. A wobbly stand, but a stand.

I rested again, hunched over, and panting heavily with my gaze fixed on the blood and dirt-stained clothing.

Scanning the area, I hunted for the easiest route up to the road. It seemed the best and safest in my condition was back behind where the car flipped off. Actually, I realize now that I was pushed. Purposely. By … I don't know who … yet. It still wasn't going to be easy by any means, but the degree of slope was much less than where the car had come down and there were more trees to use as climbing aides.

The climb would have been easy for anyone else. Much of the sharp pains faded into a huge dose of stiffness and soreness. Still extreme, but at least manageable enough to allow me to take very slow steps. Though even the slightest slip on the hike up would send an excruciating pulse right through me. Each time that happened, I'd have to rest for a minute, taking deep breaths before continuing. Every foot placement had to be precise and solid. This was especially difficult since I couldn't take full steps due to the banged knee and whatever hip damage the bullet caused. Keeping my thoughts on the task at hand, I strived for one small achievement at a time.

Without those trees to grab onto, I don't know if I would've made it. My path was at an angle along the mountainside. I couldn't simply go at it straight up. I had to cover more ground overall, but it was my only way.

Just before advancing to the point where my head was even with the road, I stopped for a moment. Letting my hand feel my lower back one more time, I felt for any fresh blood. None there. I was hesitant for the next wound, but I then pressed at my side on my hip. Turning my palm, fresh blood was evident.

Deadly Mistake

I had to see the damage. See how bad, so I carefully lifted my blouse. I was scared to see and I almost closed my eyes. The lower section of my blouse was mostly red with only a few patches of the original white color here and there. Under the blouse, various degrees of dried and crusty blood along with the newer, fresh fluid had covered my skin along with the waistband of my pants. The deep red coating over my flesh had begun to crack and flake off where my blouse had been brushing against it. Just above the pants, by about an inch, I saw it. A jagged hole about the size of a dime with a fresh little puddle of blood sitting there, growing and waiting for gravity to take hold and drag the droplet down to my pants. Three tiny flaps of skin protruded outward. I dared not touch it or attempt to press the flaps in.

The exit hole. It was where the bullet came out. I'd seen this once ... on my dad. He'd come home with a gunshot on the edge of his thigh one night. Said he was out with friends shooting at a target range and a buddy dropped his little three-eighty pistol and it went off, hitting Dad in the leg. It was odd, instead of going to a hospital, he called a doctor at midnight and the doctor came over within minutes and sewed Dad up. Asked Dad how he had been and what's new, general conversation like no big deal while he was sewing. Then left. Didn't leave a bill or anything.

I took in the scene around me for the first time. The mountains around me comprised of rocks, scattered trees, and dirt in every direction. The blue sky with absolutely no clouds could have been a picture right out of a magazine. Behind and below me, my car appeared as a crushed child's toy in the distance.

Finally, I stepped onto the edge of the black asphalt road. I made one last glance down at what was left of the silver rental car that could have easily been my coffin.

It was at that moment I realized that my cell phone was still down there. No sense in trying to go back for it. At least I'd already left Daniel the message about the accident. But that was before it became apparent that the crash was no accident.

My mind wandered. What would happen when those two men learn that I'm still alive? They'd look for me and that's for sure. Try to finish the job. Fix their mistake. For now, though, they think their mission was a success and the longer they think I'm dead, the better.

Then, the thoughts hit me, *I can't let Daniel or the girls know.* Whoever had been watching me, had most likely been watching them too. And still was.

Pictures of my husband and two little girls ran through my head. Daniel, with his blue jeans and button-up shirts. His horn-rimmed glasses and neat brown hair. He always thought the blue jeans made his shirts and sweaters look less nerdy. I used to tell him that he looked like Clark Kent before turning into Superman. Mattie and Olivia's huge smiles always made my day. Olivia's eyes more serious to reflect her personality. Mattie, like me, a little more careless. I see the newspaper pic from the refrigerator door in my mind. The one the reporter took after he bought two boxes of Girl Scout cookies from their homemade stand in the park. The girls' long brown hair nearly matching their vests.

I let those images fade away as I focused on the moment.

The police? Should I go to them? *No, not yet. Not without knowing more. Think, Kaitlyn, think.*

Someone wanted me dead. And I was pretty positive it wasn't those two in the white pickup. They were the hired thugs. That's all they were. Yeah, someone wanted me dead and I needed to figure out who. But first, I required some medical attention.

I began to limp in the direction of town. Still thinking. Still hurting.

After maybe fifty yards of my slow pace using the road's white line as my guide, I heard a vehicle in the distance. I could tell that it hadn't made the curve yet due to the displaced sound. Sounds tend to bounce off of the mountains.

I knew as soon as it cleared the curve, the driver would see me. At this stage, I could only hope it was someone with a heart.

A truck, I could tell by the rough tires on the asphalt. I quickly turned my head to look. No, not the white one. I let out a relieved breath. It was an old blue single cab Dodge. A full bench seat, judging by the four heads showing in the windshield. Two adults and two kids. I faced the truck and held out my arm, thumb in the air. Carefully watching the driver's reaction for any clue, my body rigid.

The truck's flashers came on and as it pulled closer, I could make out the flannel shirt and trucker-style baseball cap on the driver. He pulled to a stop next to me. He was an older man and possibly his mate, an old woman, was against the passenger door with a little girl and boy stuffed in the middle between them.

The aged truck idled roughly and the passenger window was already down.

I saw the lady's eyes scan me from top to bottom with an honest, but worried, expression.

"Oh my, you're hurt," were her first words. I hadn't seen how bad my face was, but if it was anything like my arms, then I must have appeared in bad shape. I already knew how bad the bloody white blouse was.

"I am," I said, "but I'll live. Could I bother you for a ride into town to the hospital?"

She turned to the man and his eyes went over the already full truck cab. He calculated the available space between them and then craned his neck up and over to see my clothes through the passenger truck window and I knew what he was thinking. I would have been thinking the same.

I spoke up loud enough so he could hear. "Let me ride in the truck bed, please. I have some bad cuts and I don't want to be a burden."

He had been silent and finally he spoke. "What happened to you, ma'am?" His eyes still studying me.

I made a motion with my arm toward the road behind us. "Oh, my car got a flat on one of the side roads back there. And stupid me, when I got out and walked around the car, I got too close to the edge of the road. The loose rocks gave way and I fell about twenty feet down into some trees." He was nodding like it made sense to him. Nearly every road around there had a drop-off ledge on one side or the other. I looked down at my own blouse and said, "It looks much worse than it is, but I do need to go get checked out."

His wife said to him quietly, but loud enough for me to hear, "Harold, she can't ride in the back. She's hurt. She …"

I interrupted, "Yes ma'am, I'm in no condition to ride up front and besides, there's no room. Please, just let me climb in the back?"

Harold told her, "Sharron, we ain't got no choice. I'm not about to let you or the grandkids ride back there. And you can't drive." He spoke up to me. "Let me pull the truck up a bit more off of the road here." I stepped out of the way as he shifted the truck into gear with a metallic *thump*.

Harold pulled past me and over the white line into the small space between the vertical cliff and asphalt. The kids twisted in the bench seat to glare through the back glass and Harold got out, walking briskly to me and the truck's tailgate. The look on his face took on a concerned, but doubtful expression as he whispered, "Lady, I don't believe that nonsense about you falling down off of any road. There ain't no side road for five miles of here. Now, I'm not gonna ask you what happened. But if you're in trouble, I can call the police for you." With a loud *clank*, he unlatched the tailgate and let it drop slowly. "You got me a little worried about you."

I smiled, "There's no need to call the police, mister." There wasn't any use in lying to him anymore, but I wasn't going to share further information either. He knew it and slapped the tailgate with the palm of his hand and said, "Ok, see if you can get yourself in here and we'll get you to the hospital."

I barely managed to slide in on my left side without yelling my lungs out while he stood there watching me, disbelieving my story about a stupid fall. It took a couple minutes, but I squirmed myself all the way inside the truck bed up against the driver's side rear wheel well.

He shook his head, staring at the side of my red-stained blouse covering the bullet's exit wound. The loud slam of the tailgate made me jump and he returned to the cab, still shaking his head.

I'd no idea how far I had driven southeast from Aspen when I was run off the road, but the ride back in the bed of the bumpy old truck was a long one. Whether it was the distance or just the pain, it felt like forever. I had wedged my hand between my butt and the hard truck bed to provide myself some cushion, and still my jaw clamped shut for just about every bump. The man, Harold, didn't believe my story. He made that clear. So, every so often, I'd look to the back window to make sure he or Sharron didn't have a phone in their hands.

Once, my eyes met the little girl's eyes and she quickly spun back around in the seat. Curious eyes. Innocent eyes. Those were my own eyes long ago.

chapter six

Aspen Valley Hospital came into sight as Harold slowly made the last left turn off of Main Street. I only remember the street name because I had been reading every sign and storefront we passed in an effort to keep my mind busy and off of the obvious.

Harold chose his path into the hospital drive carefully avoiding the potholes and bumps. Pulling up to the emergency entrance, I saw him say something to Sharron and I started to slide myself toward the tailgate before the truck came to a stop. With a bump, both me and the old Dodge seemed to huff out a sigh of relief. Sharron hopped out of the truck much faster than I'd imagine a lady her age would have and proceeded through the automatic doors.

My eyes followed her in and to the desk where she got the attention of a lady in scrubs.

The loud sound of the tailgate latch gave me my cue to work my body across those last couple feet. Harold stood nearby just in case, but never touched me.

Working my way out until my legs hung over the tailgate with my toes barely scraping the concrete below, I took a breath and let myself slip off. The immense pain in my rear when my body weight rubbed across the blunt, hard edge of the tailgate lip during my slide literally made me forget that my legs might not be their best either.

They gave way. The legs. Both of them. I collapsed onto the concrete like a stuffed animal. Harold yelled to the nurse and Sharron who had just come out of the doors with a wheel chair, "Hurry! She fell. She fell." He leaned over me and apologized, "I'm sorry, Miss. I'm sorry."

I winced, motionless on the cold concrete, waiting for the hurt to fade away some. Lying in a bundle under the back of the truck, I said, "It's ok, Mr. Harold. Don't worry."

My eyes were still closed when I felt a hand on my shoulder. "I'm a nurse. Kathy. Are you ok to move? Do you think you can get into this chair?"

"Yes, just give me a second." I opened my eyes and rolled over to my back, looking up at the underside of the open tailgate. The letters that spelled Dodge had been chipped and faded over time. The lower section was no longer blue. It was mostly rust.

"Do I need to move the truck up?" asked Harold.

I could tell the nurse was getting ready to say yes to him when I said, "No, wait, Mr. Harold. I can grab hold of the tailgate to help me up. I'm coming, people." The nurse nodded in agreement, but her eyes showed disbelief.

I pushed up into a sitting position and reached to the tailgate's lip. The nurse, seeing I was actually going to try it, took hold of me under one arm and lifted as I pulled.

The nurse's eyes went to my blouse when I lowered myself into the wheelchair. I noticed the kids in the truck leaning over the bench seat, watching everything, and gave them a wink and then focused on Harold. "Mr. Harold … and Mrs. Sharron, thank you so much for giving me the ride. I'm sorry for bothering you, but I do thank you."

Sharron smiled with a tilted head. "You take care, ok," she said and turned back to the truck. She motioned for the kids to spin around and get settled into place.

Harold stood near and after Sharron had closed the truck door, he leaned forward some, touching me for the first time by laying his hand across the top of mine gently, and said, "You be careful. Get whatever help you need. If you are ever in a bind again, you look us up, Harold Weeks. We're in the phone book."

I felt the chair rolling backwards, turn and then proceed to the automatic doors. Nurse Kathy was at the helm and she said, "We need to get you checked in and you can tell me exactly what happened to you."

As we reached the doors and they glided open, I simply said, "Gunshot."

Kathy leaned forward. "I'm sorry, what did you say?"

"Gunshot," I repeated, "that's what happened to me. Gunshot."

Nurse Kathy didn't say anything more but picked up her pace, rushing me through the doors. She rolled me into the waiting area where I immediately scanned the room. A middle-aged man was holding his shoulder, leaning to the side in one of the fabric covered chairs on the middle row. Two rows of chairs over was an elderly couple. The man appeared fine, but his lady did not. His wife, I'd presume. Her oxygen tube stretched behind her and to the floor where a black bag was set.

I stared at her while Kathy parked me at the very end of a row near the check-in desk. The elderly lady looked like, well, she looked like her time was running out. Her husband held her hand and even though she only gazed at the tan carpet below her, his attention was focused on her. Love. His face shone with it. Worry and unconditional love.

Nurse Kathy disappeared behind a white door after pressing a code into a keypad. I twisted around to take note of any other surroundings. Behind me, to my left, were the automatic entry doors and a big wall of windows. The old blue Dodge was just turning onto Main Street and I watched it disappear.

My body relaxed and a tiredness came over me as I waited for Kathy's return. Letting my eyelids fall shut, my breathing slowed and I felt as if I could have gone to sleep right there. It worried me, though. Was it fatigue or was it blood loss causing the drowsiness? I doubted it was blood loss. I'd be passed out or dead already if the gunshot was that bad or the placement had been better.

A loud *thud* sound shook me. It was from when a car hits a curb wrong and the back tire, shocks, or struts make that distinct sound. I'm no mechanic, but I knew the sound. Just outside of the large windows, I saw the white truck. It could have been any white truck, of course. But this one rounded the parking lot corner fast and with a mission. The driver had taken the corner too sharp and the back passenger tire jumped the curb. A white truck, four doors, and tinted windows ... just like the truck that ran me off of the mountain.

My stare followed the truck through the parking lot and into a parking space near the back of the lot.

I held my breath.

Watching ... waiting ...

The passenger side door opened first. When he stepped out, I saw the slicked-back dark hair.

It was him.

It was them.

I felt a tap on my shoulder and looked up to nurse Kathy standing there with her clipboard and some guy in a white lab coat with a stethoscope hanging from around his neck. Nurse Kathy said, "This is Dr. Maddox ..."

I didn't hear the rest. My attention was on the two men walking from the truck. They stopped briefly in the middle of the parking lot, scoping out the two entrances. Besides the emergency entrance, there was another, the main hospital one.

Dr. Maddox noticed my lack of interest to him and asked, "Miss, can you hear me? Please look at me."

I didn't.

The two in the parking lot decided to split up. The slicked-back dark-haired guy came toward the emergency room entrance and his partner went to the main hospital one.

Without even thinking, my hands went to the armrests of the wheelchair and I pushed. Pushed hard. I flew out of the chair right between nurse Kathy and the Dr. Maddox man.

My legs didn't work again and I hit the floor. Face first. Dr. Maddox just stood there in shock of the immediate change in the current situation and Nurse Kathy squatted down to help me up, but I was already gaining traction and once I got my feet up underneath me, I pushed into to a stand and bolted to the white door with the keypad. I twisted the handle with all my might, but it didn't budge. It was locked. Nurse Kathy was right behind me pressing the keypad buttons. A low *beep* sounded and I yanked the handle down, pulling the door open.

Looking back, I saw the dark-haired guy still about fifty feet or so away from the entrance. I rushed through the doorway with nurse Kathy on my heels, letting the door shut behind us.

She grabbed my arm, pulling me to the side, "Here, this exam room."

It wasn't really a room, more of a sectioned off area with a bed and one of those rolling curtain things. In one quick motion, she tugged the curtain around us, shielding the room from the door's small window.

I heard two voices near the white door, then all went quiet.

The door opened. Footsteps toward us. Then the voice of Dr. Maddox, "Kathy, are you in here?"

"Yes, Doctor," she replied.

He parted the curtain only enough to enter.

I leaned up against the bed awkwardly in an attempt to get weight off of my feet with the hope that it would ease the throb coming from my right hip.

"Kathy said you have a gunshot wound." It was more of a statement than a question.

"Yes," I answered.

"Was it the man that came in here who shot you?"

"I don't know," was my answer even though I knew different.

Dr. Maddox peered at me in disbelief. The same look that Harold had given me. He asked, "What's your name, Miss?"

I said, "I don't remember."

He asked, "Do you remember being shot?"

"No." This wasn't going so well.

"That man in the lobby was looking for someone of your description. He said he heard his sister had been shot by accident out at their family cabin. Is this true?"

"Maybe."

Dr. Maddox's expression changed and he said, "Ok, we'll get to those details in a minute then. Most importantly, I need to check you out." He traced my body with his eyes and settled in on lower part of my blouse. "Can you turn around, please?" Reaching to the box on the wall, he pulled out two blue-colored exam gloves and slipped one on.

I braced myself with my hands on the surface of the clean, white exam bed and twisted my backside around to he and Kathy. My face toward the wall. Nurse Kathy stood silent. I heard the other glove make a *snap* sound as he put it on. I felt my blouse lift. The cool hospital air rushed across my skin.

Just to the right of my spine, the doctor pushed in tenderly with his finger and let go. I winced. A much lighter touch tapped on the exit wound a couple times.

"Is this the only one?" he asked.

"Only gunshot?"

"Correct," he said.

"Yes."

He continued, "We will need to get your information and get a CT as soon as possible."

"No," I said.

"What do you mean, 'no'?"

I repeated, "No. Just give me a rough idea if this is a major injury or not. Will it heal?"

I twisted my body back around and leaned up on the bed again. "Will it heal? Is it major?"

Poor Kathy looked lost. She glanced back and forth from me to the doctor.

Dr. Maddox crossed his arms. "Do you remember anything?"

"No."

He shuffled his feet on the slick floor looking down at them. "So, you either don't remember anything or you won't tell me anything. Is that right?"

"Yes. That's right."

He appeared to be thinking very hard. There were rules and laws for handling things in the medical field. I didn't know them. But they did exist. I could see in his face that he didn't believe anything I had said. Standing there and not saying a word, he was driving me crazy. Finally, he uttered, "I think it'll heal. The bullet made a shallow entrance under the skin with a clean exit. Honestly, you'd be near death by now if any vitals were struck. We can clean it and sew it up. I won't ask anymore questions."

I relaxed. "Then why do I feel the huge throb back here?" I reached back, lifted my blouse, and touched with my finger the area between the two wounds.

"Turn back around, please," he ordered.

He applied direct pressure where I pointed. It hurt. He pressed with either one or two fingers and the pain shot through me. I grunted loudly.

"Ok, you can turn around," he said. "I'd feel much better doing a CT. Will you give me your information? Name and insurance?"

"No."

He sighed and walked to the trashcan while removing the gloves off of his hands. "I am guessing the bullet grazed your iliac crest. The fact that you are walking tells me that it isn't shattered."

"The what?" I asked.

He returned from the trashcan and said, "The very top of your pelvis. I imagine the bullet caused some damage there, hopefully minimal since you are foregoing a scan."

"Will it heal?"

Dr. Maddox nodded his head with no verbal reply.

Nurse Kathy, who hadn't moved through the entire ordeal asked the doctor, "What do we do?"

"Clean her, stitch her, and let her go." Dr. Maddox then said to me, "I'd normally keep anyone here who was claiming amnesia. However, I'm a little skeptical of your lack of memory." He shook his head and asked, "Shall I contact the authorities?"

"No. Not yet. I can't right now. You have to understand." I kept eye contact with him through my words and into the long seconds of silence that followed.

"Very well," he told me as he disappeared through the curtain.

chapter seven

Daniel sat at the kitchen table with his arms crossed and his cell phone right in front of him. His laptop just beyond the phone and open to the American Airlines webpage.

Olivia darted through the kitchen to the refrigerator. "What're you doing, Daddy?"

The girls thought their mother was still on the business trip out west. That was the only information that Daniel had shared with them so far. He smiled at Olivia and said, "I'm waiting on a phone call."

Olivia slammed the fridge door. "From Mom?"

That question stabbed deep inside him. He adjusted his glasses. "No, babe, only a business call."

The phone vibrated on the table, giving off a loud buzz, then it rang. Daniel said to Olivia, "Ok, why don't you go play now. I've got to answer this." She flew out of the kitchen with a soda in her hand nearly as fast as she had run in.

He had already saved the number in his contacts and the screen read Aspen Police Dept. His hand shook as he picked the phone up. "Hello, this is Daniel Cline. Did you find her?"

The female voice on the other end said, "Mr. Cline, I'm sorry, but we have not."

"How about her car? Did you find that?"

"No, Mr. Cline, I had two units out today on Highway 82 looking."

"And? Nothing?"

"No, my officers did not find the car. I will have them out again tomorrow."

"She is wrecked somewhere near you. Why can't you find her?"

"Mr. Cline," the officer on the phone was trying her best, "are you certain that your wife was driving out of Aspen? Could she have been in a different town instead?"

"She said she was in Aspen!" shouted Daniel. "You don't believe me! Dammit, she's there somewhere." His eyes began to water.

Olivia and Mattie slowly tip-toed into the hall from their rooms. "Daddy," Mattie said. "Is Mom ok?"

Daniel covered the phone with the palm of his hand. "Yes, Mom's fine. Go on now," he said and motioned with his hand for the girls to return to their room.

"Mr. Cline," the officer said in a manner questioning if he was still on the line and listening.

"Yes, I'm still here."

"Mr. Cline, I'll have officers out again first thing in the morning. If she's here, we'll find her."

"Ok, let me know as soon as you do, please."

"I will."

Daniel hung up the phone and pulled the laptop closer. He'd already found a flight and had it saved waiting on that call. He hit the enter button and the screen flashed a message stating that his flight has been reserved.

"Girls," he said loudly.

They immediately popped their heads out since they'd been eavesdropping from the edge of their doors. "What Dad?" asked Olivia.

"I'm going to take a trip for a few days and you'll stay at your Granny's." He hated keeping things from them. They were old enough to understand that something *was* wrong. But Daniel wasn't ready to even admit it to himself.

It was early morning and Daniel was sitting at the airport waiting for his flight announcement to board the plane. The sun had only recently broken across the horizon. A golf magazine was on the chair next to him and his only suitcase, a carry-on, was at his feet on the floor. He'd tried to flip through the magazine to get his mind off of the unknown, but it didn't work and he had given it up.

The buzz of his phone startled him and he yanked it out of his pocket, hoping to see the screen let him know Kaitlyn was calling. Instead, it read Aspen Police Dept. "Yes, Daniel here," he answered quickly.

"Mr. Cline, we had a call from a resident very late last night."

"Did you find her?" interrupted Daniel.

"No. The rental car has been located. And her cell phone," said the officer.

"But not her?"

"No, Mr. Cline. We are thinking that she may have taken refuge overnight at a resident's home nearby. Knocking on doors is our next step."

Daniel shifted his weight forward in the airport seat, leaning his elbows onto his knees. "Did you check the hospital? She may have ended up there."

"We have already contacted the hospital and questioned about any possible car wreck patients that match your wife's description."

"Nothing?"

"No, Mr. Cline."

A voice came over the speaker, "American Airlines flight number 323 to Denver, Colorado is now boarding."

Daniel stood up, grabbing his carry-on. He told the officer on the phone, "Ok, I'm heading there now. Please let me know of anything new."

"We will, Mr. Cline."

chapter eight

After checking me out, cleaning me, and finally sewing up the entrance and exit wounds of the bullet, Nurse Kathy volunteered to take me to her home for the night. Dr. Maddox seemed hesitant when she mentioned it to him, but from a distance I saw him nod. He told her something in a low voice, too low for me to hear. I already knew that he was positive I was lying about not knowing what my name was and the rest of the story, so I bet he told her to try and find out. We discarded my blouse and pants into the biohazard trash and clothed me in one of those ever-so-comfy and beautiful hospital gowns with Kathy's promise that she'd loan me something better at her house. I made sure to discretely tuck my little coin wallet that contained my ID, some cash and cards into my undies unnoticed.

Kathy had a very nice, small townhome on the outskirts of town. She was such a sweet soul. Thankfully, the entrance to her townhome was on the floor level. I was feeling much better, either from the care or from the handful of Tylenol. I'm sure I'll know which in a couple more hours.

She didn't really ask me anything on the trip there, only chit-chat about the weather and … *how they say we'll have an early winter and that the ski season might even open in late October this year.*

I tried to oblige, smile, and act interested. However, my thoughts kept returning to those two men. *Why me?* I worked as a low-level Assistant District Attorney in North Carolina. Nothing fancy, nothing crazy, nothing dangerous. Hell, I only worked small-time stuff, misdemeanors, petty theft, things like that.

Kathy opened the door to the townhome and gestured for me to go on in. There were lovely wood floors leading through a small living room to the kitchen at the far end. It had big windows that let gobs of light in and gave an amazing view of the mountains. I was walking better. One helluva limp, but walking at least.

"Go get comfortable on the sofa and rest. Can I get you something to drink?" she asked.

I was terribly thirsty. "Water please." I settled into the cushy sofa seat slowly and carefully.

I heard the ice cubes click against each other in the glass, then she asked, "Bottle water or tap?"

"Tap is fine," I answered.

From the sink, she looked at me. "So, what should I call you? Can you remember your name yet?"

I grinned, accepting her fact-finding motives and also thinking of what to tell her. "Just call me Allie."

"Is that your real name? Are you remembering?" she questioned.

"No, I'm not remembering. I've just always liked that name." I closed my eyes. Images of my mother popped into my mind. Her name was Alexandra and Dad always called her Allie. I think most people shorten that name actually.

Kathy walked to me with the glass of water with the ice cubes jingling inside. "Well, here you go, Allie. I'll hunt up some better stuff for you to wear."

A sincere laugh snuck out of me and I said, "Yes, that'd be great. This gown and I are getting tired of each other."

I'd been through so much in one day. The fatigue was finally catching up. I still couldn't believe someone tried to kill me. Or, let me correct that, was still trying to kill me. I wished so bad that I could talk to Daniel and the girls. Let them know I was ok. I knew Daniel'd be going crazy and I hoped he got the message I'd left him and it made some sort of sense. I was so dazed when I made that call.

And … I wished I'd had a weapon when that guy started shooting at me. Damn, I only wish. Dad taught me to use a pistol when I was younger. He'd bring me out to a private range owned by some guy he knew. His friend was ex-military, Special Forces or something like that. I was good. I was accurate. I was fast. I even competed until my early twenties.

"They're not the best, but these should be more comfortable than what you've got on now. Hope you like the Denver Broncos," Kathy said as she brought a pair of jeans and a Broncos t-shirt.

"I like that Broncos shirt way better than this hospital gown."

She didn't hand them to me immediately. She bundled them up in her lap, sat down next to me on the sofa and turned her body sideways to face me. "Any luck? You know, remembering anything?"

"No, I'm sorry."

"Do you remember that last place you were? Before you got in the back of the pickup truck?"

I shook me head. "Maybe tomorrow after some rest."

She reached out and placed her hand on my knee. "I'm worried. People don't just come in everyday with gunshot wounds and not know how they got them. That guy, the one you ran from. He told Dr. Maddox that he was your brother. Is that true?"

"Kathy, I really don't know," I answered. She was fishing hard for information.

"Why did you freak out when you saw him?"

"I don't know. Instinct. Maybe something in my subconscious. I don't have an answer." My main worry was that she'd start calling people as her next step. I realized that I had to tempt her with some bait. "I do have small flashes of a scene. But I can't make anything of it."

"Tell me what you see."

I looked into her eyes as serious as I could and started making up a story. "I can see myself holding a gun, a pistol. Somewhere in the mountains. Just me. By myself. That's it. Maybe I was shooting targets. Maybe I dropped the gun and fell after the shot and that's why ..." I looked down at the floor and closed my eyes. "After that, it's all fuzzy. Maybe in the morning after a good night's sleep."

I felt her fingers tapping my knee. "Ok, hun, get some rest and hopefully tomorrow by the time I get back from work, your memory may have cleared up a little more and you'll remember your name or a family member, something."

"I'm so sorry for being all this trouble."

She stood up and set the clothes on the sofa. Glancing to a clock in the kitchen, she said, "I have a twelve-hour shift starting bright and early at seven. I need to go take a bath and get some rest myself. I had my supper at work before you showed up, but I bet you are starving." She pointed to the kitchen. "Feel free to help yourself to anything. There's some leftovers in the fridge and other food in the cabinets. Just help yourself and I'll see you when I get back tomorrow evening."

"Thank you," I said, smiling at her generosity.

She patted the sofa with her hand. "This is all I've got for you to sleep on. It's a small place. I'll grab some blankets, though."

Sleep came fast and hard. I dreamt of a time that I purposely try not to think of. Back from when my mom was alive. In the dream, I was about eleven or twelve. Mom was sitting in a chair against the wall at the dojo. We were in my old taekwondo class. Mom used to tell me that a girl should to know how to defend herself.

The dream was of me sparring with a boy. We were in all of our pads. Mom watched intently from her chair. The boy swung hard with his right fist. But his face wasn't that of a boy. It was a man's face and he swung hard, like a man. I ducked the strike and dropped to the floor, sweeping his leg out from under him. And when he fell, he disappeared. He was gone. I looked over to my mom's chair and it was empty. She was gone.

The morning sunlight coming from the big windows was terribly bright. I pulled the blanket all the way over my head and tried to bring back the dream. I desperately wanted to see Mom's face again. Even if it was just a dream. I began to cry, thinking of my girls coming to the realization that *I* was gone. The emotional me said that I couldn't do that to them. I had to let them know I was ok. I had to. Emotional me told me that Daniel and the twins deserved to know. But rational me said not to, not yet anyway.

Still under the blanket, I turned my head toward the kitchen and slowly slid the blanket down just enough so I could see the clock on the kitchen counter. 9:06am.

Everything on me ached. The direct pain had faded away overnight, but I was sore all over.

I emerged from my blanket and slipped on the jeans and Broncos shirt, then neatly folded the blanket. The deep down urge to call Daniel was strong. I couldn't risk it, though. I'd already decided that, sort of. My dad. That was who I needed to call. And … I needed to get out of Kathy's townhome. Kathy had been the best, but I couldn't rule out the fact that she may call the police from work, especially after that doctor asked about me.

My mind was thinking more clearly than yesterday, but I was still sure I needed to remain as invisible as possible for the time-being. I ran different scenarios in my mind. With police involved, whoever hired my hit could simply crawl back into their cave and disappear until the smoke blew over. Then they'd just try to finish the job at a later time, probably succeeding at that. If I went home to Daniel and the girls, I'd put my whole family at risk. I'd never been in this big of a mess before and I truly didn't know what to do. But Dad might know.

After tidying up the sofa, I went to the bathroom to check the bullet wounds and other scratches. All looked good. My face and arms still looked like I lost a fight with a big cat.

Leaving the bathroom, I saw Kathy had also left out an old pair of Converse shoes with a fresh pair of socks on the kitchen counter with a note. The note read, *Take it easy and rest. I'll bring dinner after I get off work. Try these shoes, they might fit.*

The note made me smile. I pulled my coin purse out of the front pocket of the jeans and dug out the cash I had in there, eighty-two dollars total. Flipping her note over, I wrote with a pen I found in a one of the drawers, *Kathy, I thank you immensely for all you've done for me. I must leave, though. Here's some money for the clothes. Thanks, Allie.* The letter "A" in Allie wasn't quite written correctly since I nearly started the name with a "K." I left sixty dollars on the note, put the shoes and socks on and walked out, locking her door behind me.

The next priority was to find a phone to call Dad. I didn't dare call from Kathy's townhome. Leaving her place and stepping out into the town had an eerie feeling about it. I was in the open. I was prey. Someone still hunted for me and I wouldn't know if each face I came across was someone who was after me or not.

I walked toward downtown past rows and rows of townhomes and condos. It was a busy place. Kids on skateboards and people walking in and out of every entrance. Some looked like tourists and others looked like they could be locals. I avoided making eye contact with any of them. What I was looking for was some sort of office or reception area that was staffed. About ten blocks toward town, I finally saw a hotel sign. Picking up my pace, I headed there in hopes that I could talk my way into use of a phone, a basic landline.

Before closing the door behind me, I glanced around at the people outside. None of them appeared to be paying any attention to my goings.

"Good morning, do you have a reservation?" the guy asked as I entered. The classy decor and patterned carpet gave the impression that it was a pricey place. The little guy had on an actual uniform with a shiny brass name badge. I gave no consideration to the name.

"No, I don't have a reservation. I want to ask if I can use a phone around here for a private call." I watched his expression, not sure of how this would play out.

"Are you a current guest with us?"

"No, I'm not. I just need to use a phone."

He squinted his eyes, shook his head, and said, "I'm very sorry, ma'am. All phone use is reserved for our guests. You could try ..." He was blowing me off.

Pulling my coin purse out, I retrieved a ten dollar bill and set it on his counter. "Could I rent a phone maybe?"

He looked side to side, then leaned awkwardly across the counter, casually covering the bill with his right elbow. I noticed the security camera over his left shoulder and realized he was purposely blocking the view. He murmured, "Go through those double doors and in the back corner of the room is a phone on the wall. Dial nine to get out if it's long distance."

"Thanks," I said and pushed my way through the doors leading into what was the make-shift breakfast area for the guests' free food. The room was about half-full of hotel patrons scattered at the tables eating and chatting.

My fingers shook as I dialed the numbers. Talking to my dad about this was going to make it even more real.

"Hello," he answered.

Only my breathing and the distant sounds of metal utensils against the cheap glass dishes made their way into the phone's speaker. I had no words. I didn't know what to say. Or, how to start. It had been over six months since I'd talked to him.

"Hello, anybody there?"

In that moment, I was a little girl again, "Dad," I whispered into the phone.

"Kait, is that you?" he asked.

Tears fell down my cheeks. "Dad, yes it's me."

"Are you ok?"

"No, Dad ... I'm not?" I whispered in a shaky voice. "I'm in trouble and I don't know what to do."

"What kind of trouble, darling?" His tone was so soothing. I began to weep even more, standing there in the corner of that dark room with the fancy green and gold patterned carpet. Guilt swept over me. Guilt for not staying in touch. Guilt for not visiting. Guilt for not being a better daughter. Life just got in the way. And talking to him always brought up those memories. Memories of Mom.

"Dad, I've been shot," I said softly with my hand covering the phone's speaker. "Someone's trying to kill me."

The phone went silent.

"Are you still there?" I asked.

When Dad spoke again, the tone of his voice had changed. It was stern, strong, authoritative. "Where are you now?"

"I'm in ..." It was hard to answer him. To let him know that I was only a few hours away and hadn't contacted him or planned a visit. "I'm in Aspen. Aspen, Colorado." I waited for him to say something in regards to me being so close. The line was silent.

"Ok, I'll come get you. Hold on a minute, let me look something up," he said.

Some of the guests were moving around in the little breakfast lounge dumping their plates and making their way out. I counted five that had left while I'd been talking. None of them had seemed to even notice me.

Dad came back on the line. "It looks like there's only one Starbucks in town. A few blocks south of Main."

"Ok."

"It will take me over six hours to get there from here in Farmington. Can you hold out and stay unnoticed until I get there?"

"Yes."

"Fine. I'll pick you up at the Starbucks in roughly seven hours."

"Hey, Dad."

"What?" he asked.

I watched the last couple leave the lounge through the double doors. "Thanks ... I love you."

"Love you too. Stay outta sight."

"I will." I heard the *click* on his end and I reached back, hanging my receiver up.

chapter nine

Daniel parked the rental car and checked his watch. He made a mental note of the current time, 12:28pm, just after noon, mountain time. He'd driven roughly four and a half hours from the Denver airport where his plane had landed just after 8:00am. A few valuable minutes' time was killed at a gas station waiting on a breakfast burrito after filling up. Only noon, but it had already been a long day considering two hours had disappeared due to the time zone change.

Turning the car off, he stared at the big letters, ASPEN POLICE. It was summer, but there was a coolness to the air when he opened the car door. Being used to the humid and hot eastern weather, the mountains of Colorado was huge change.

Officer Cantrell. That was who he had been talking with and who he was to meet. When Daniel entered, an officer standing at a counter on the opposite wall turned around. "How can I help you?" he asked.

"I'm here to see Officer Cantrell." Daniel let his eyes take in the nice new station. Various mountain images and motifs adorned the brick walls. Behind the counter was a big Aspen Police logo with a gold aspen tree leaf prominently placed between the two words.

The officer at the counter smiled and said, "I'll get her. Just wait here, please."

So many questions spun around in Daniel's mind, but he tried to keep them at bay by pacing around the station. Daniel hadn't been in many stations in his life, but the ones he had been in tended to be old, drab buildings with dark paneling from the late seventies and faded florescent bulbs that flickered in the ceilings under their old and yellowed light coverings.

This station was so much different. It was bright, inviting. The huge windows let in an enormous amount of natural light and gave wonderful views of the city along with the distant mountains.

The sounds of footsteps were followed by a woman's voice. "Mr. Cline, I'm Stephanie Cantrell."

Daniel extended his right hand to accept the customary shake. "Hi, just call me Daniel."

"Sure. Daniel, I wish we were meeting under better circumstances."

"Me as well. Is there anything new?"

"Yes. There are some new developments. But nothing major," she said.

"Haven't found Kaitlyn yet, though?" he asked in a depressed voice.

"No, we have not found her."

Daniel shoved his hands into his pockets and let his shoulders slump. "Have you gotten the car yet? Or Kaitlyn's stuff from it? I'd like to see whatever I can. Maybe, just maybe, there might be something useful in there."

"We have arrangements with the road crew to shut down Highway 82 at three o'clock today. We'll use a winch truck to pull the car up and load it onto a wrecker." She paused. "Mr. Cline, I went out earlier this morning to the scene. It was a very far tumble that your wife took off of the side of the mountain."

"What are you not telling me?"

"Mr. Cline, there's quite a bit of blood inside the car. It looks like she had a very rough fall. Myself and another officer searched the immediate area and can see where it appears she may have been thrown from or exited the car after the wreck."

Daniel intently listened without a word.

Officer Cantrell continued, "We did not find her. I did, however, send officers to question more neighbors and check the hospital again."

Daniel began to sway as his mind wrapped around the details. "… and nothing? No sign of her?"

"No sir." Officer Cantrell was used to the awkwardness of situations like this. Her training had prepared her for the uncomfortable. She stood silent, letting Daniel take it all in. "Mr. Cline," she said, "you can ride with one of the officers out to the scene if you'd like."

"Yeah," Daniel said with a slight nod. "Yeah, I need to see it. To see the place."

"Ok, be back here at two-thirty," she said. "And Daniel, I still have a feeling that she may have made it to someone's home for help."

"Then why haven't you gotten a call from them? It doesn't make any sense to me?"

"Daniel," said Officer Cantrell in her most comforting of tones, "in these mountains, we do still have many people here who live off the grid. Even these days. No phones or internet. I've even met some who prefer to have absolutely no contact with anyone. It has been one full day since you notified us of the wreck and I have two officers checking other homes in the area that we missed this morning."

Daniel nodded again. Not to the officer, but more to himself. "Sure. I'll go grab some food and coffee."

Walking out of the station, Daniel noticed how much his rental car stood out. Like it was yelling for attention. A bright red Dodge Charger. He'd asked for whatever was cheapest, and the rental car lady told him he had two options, the fire-engine red Charger or an extra cab pickup.

Upon arriving back at the station, Daniel was introduced to the officer that he'd ride out to the scene with. He shook hands and went through the formal name exchanges, but the words were a blur and only faded into the air. His mind was only on Kaitlyn.

Daniel stared out of the patrol car's window through town and eventually southeast on Highway 82. It was the last road his wife had been on. A curvy road from the start, with a mountain on the left side and drop-offs in many places on the right.

The right.

The passenger side.

His side.

Curiosity made him look down, but nausea urged him to keep his focus ahead. *Kaitlyn could be anywhere down there*, he thought. He let his eyes focus on each side road they passed, wishing he'd see her walking along one of them.

The patrol car slowed coming into the final left curve, coasting around the few idling cars with very confused drivers in them, wondering why their southbound progress had come to an abrupt halt. The lead car was being held in place by an orange cone. Just beyond the cone, a road worker held up a STOP sign on a pole. He stood on the white line, and only a few inches past the heels of his boots, the highway dropped off. He gave a flick of his wrist letting the officer and Daniel know that they could proceed.

The highway curved left, but the view was blocked by the mountainside. It wasn't a sharp turn, but a long and gradual curve. Daniel leaned forward in his seat, looking ahead and down to the right, noticing how the drop-off seemed to flirt with the white line on highway pavement, almost touching in some spots.

They slowed and came to a stop. A hundred feet in front was a large tow truck. Or winch truck. Regardless, Daniel saw the roll of cable that was gradually unwinding and snaking its way over the edge of the drop-off. Opening his passenger door, Daniel gasped slightly at the sheer drop to his side.

The officer stepped out and gave Daniel his warning, "Be careful and stay out of the way."

Daniel gave no indication of even hearing the order and went directly toward the winch truck as if hypnotized. A big man in canvas coveralls at the truck controlled the motor with the cable disappearing over the edge. The motor gave off a loud whining sound and with a heavily-gloved hand, the man cautiously guided the cable as it came out.

Keeping himself at a safe distance from the truck, Daniel followed the cable to the drop-off. As he stepped closer, part of him did't want to see what was below, but he knew he had to. Once near the edge, it was visible. A silver, four-door car of some brand. Unrecognizable. There was no way to tell from the distance and in its condition. The car had the look of a crushed beer can. Another man was carefully making his way down the incline to the car, dragging the end of the cable with him. With each step, piles of rock and dirt were forced loose and sent down to the car, creating a small haze of orange dust.

Hesitantly, Daniel took the first step over the edge. His inexperience on unleveled ground showed as the rocks gave way under his foot and he slipped. His feet finally catching a grip another ten inches down.

"You can't go down there!" shouted the officer.

Daniel looked back at him. The officer had given the order but didn't give any indication that he was going to physically stop Daniel's descent. Another step and another slide on the loose rocks. His body and brain understood quickly how cautious his steps needed to be and he began to use a side-stepping motion to traverse down at an angle away from the man below. It was the best Daniel could do to keep the falling rocks from hitting him.

By the time Daniel reached the bottom near the car, the man who'd been dragging the cable had completed the hook-up. He was at the front of the car sitting on the dirt. He yanked hard on the cable and a loud metallic *snap* sounded from under the car.

Being at the scene was different than he'd expected. Daniel took heavy breaths in an attempt to keep the emotions away. He wanted to believe deep down that Kaitlyn was alive, somewhere. Both he and the Aspen Police Department just didn't know exactly where. Officer

Cantrell was still sticking by her gut feeling that Kaitlyn had made it to someone's home and they were taking care of her. But why hadn't she called? Or seek medical help? He understood the hermit theory, but it was a hard pill to swallow in this day and age. Cantrell's explanation did make some sense, but ... Kaitlyn would surely need to be checked over or something after this kind of wreck.

The car was in as bad of shape as it looked from the road. Not a single window intact. All four tires were flat, with the passenger's side front tire rotated at an odd angle. Every inch of metal had a dent, crush mark, or wrinkle. Daniel walked around it slowly, ending at the driver's side door. Inside, the dried up splatters of blood had turned a dark, deep red color, almost black against the light grey leather interior.

The wrecker man dusted off his pants as he stood and said, "Hey, we're gonna have to start pulling this up pretty soon. Ok."

"I know," answered Daniel without looking at him. Daniel ran his fingers along the driver's door, following along each new imperfection while his thoughts attempted to recreate the tumble in his mind. His fingers stopped at a small hole in the door. He squatted down. There was another hole in the metal only a few inches to the right of the first. Two perfectly round holes mixed in with all the dents and crush marks.

"Mister," said Daniel, "what's this?"

The man squatted next to Daniel, "Whatcha got?"

"These two holes," Daniel said. "What do you think they're from? What do they look like to you?"

The man stood and shrugged. "No tellin'. Those probably got there from the roll down here. That car rolled across a lot of sharp rocks coming down a drop like that. Somethin' poked through, I guess."

They both looked up behind them to the rough mountainside. Daniel let his fingers fall from the metal door. "Yeah, probably so."

"We need to start."

Daniel stuck his head inside the car through the broken window. "Ok, I'll hurry. Just looking."

"So, are you the insurance guy?"

Daniel had noticed Kaitlyn's purse on the passenger side floorboard and pulled his head out to walk around. "Huh?" he replied.

"Insurance guy? Is that who you are?"

With a straight face, Daniel answered, "No, I'm her husband."

"Oh. Oh shit, man, I'm sorry," said the man. "You can take a couple more minutes. I'll start climbing back up to the road."

Daniel stepped back away from the car, staring at it. Wishing, just wishing the car could talk. Hoping and wishing it could tell him where his wife might have gone.

Reaching up with both hands, he ran his fingers through his hair. The car became blurry as tears formed in his eyes. Daniel bit his lower lip. The tears broke away from his eyelids and dropped down to the bottom rim of his glasses one at a time.

"Mister," said the man from halfway up the mountainside.

Reaching through the passenger window and grabbing the purse, Daniel walked away from the car so the men could start tightening the cable. The cable slowly straightened against the mountainside as the slack was being pulled out and the winch motor from the truck above let out a loud, complaining *groan* upon the increased tension. Rocks started falling as Daniel began his ascent.

chapter ten

I sat at the table furthest from the door and made sure to position myself to have a clear view of each entrance. The Starbucks cup was centered on the table with my hands clasped around as if I were holding it for the warmth. I wasn't. I was only holding it for the comfort. The name *Allie* was scribbled against the white background of the cup. Two dollars and eleven cents. Paid cash. I almost paid with a card. Almost. But I remembered that I didn't want to share my name with anyone right now.

It had been nearly three years since I'd seen Dad in person. I was nervous. I was guilty. I was ashamed. And I had no valid defense for such a long time-lapse. I dreaded the look in his eyes. That was why my hands were around the coffee cup for comfort, I noticed the clock on the wall read 6:02pm.

I watched for his van. Well, I watched for the van I remember him having three years ago, the silver Honda

Odyssey. When I saw it, I'd go out to meet him and save him the trouble of unloading.

6:05pm.

6:07pm.

From the right corner of the building, I saw him. The once tall, once brown haired, once youthful and handsome man rolling his wheelchair up the concrete ramp to the door. I jumped up, went to the door and held it open.

"Hey, darling," he said with a smile as he wheeled into the building.

I greeted him in what could be called a whimper, "Hi, Dad," and let the door shut. "Here, I'm at this table. Do you want anything?"

"Well, hell yeah," he said. "That way I can at least say that I drove damned near seven hours for a cup of coffee in Aspen fucking Colorado."

Dad scooted the metal chair out of the way so he could fit his wheelchair in its spot at the table. I went to get him a coffee.

"Black and bring me some sugar," he ordered out loud.

I brought a few sugar packs with his coffee and sat across from him. He was staring at my coffee cup. "Allie," he said, "good one."

"I'm sorry, I couldn't think of anything else when I was with the nurse. It was the first name that popped into my head." I watched him for any clue.

He gave me forced smile and said, "It's fine. Fine. You look so much like her anyway, you could pass with that name and her ID." Taking a small sip of his coffee, he asked me, "So, how'd you get yourself into this?"

I glanced around the room to be sure no special attention was being given to us and opened my mouth to give an answer but ...

Dad, noticing my nervousness and obvious observations, spoke before I could answer. "Nobody's listening and no one is watching. The two to the left are talking about school, the one guy to my right flank back there is busy typing on his phone, and one of the baristas is having problems with her contact lens while the other is sitting on his ass behind that wall on a cardboard box. No one is listening. How'd you get yourself into this?"

I leaned forward to him, looking him in the eyes. "I really don't know. And by the way, do you always pay that much attention to everyone in a room?"

"Yes. I do."

He had a look on his face I'd not seen before, or maybe never really noticed. "Do you have any cases at work that could be bigger than they seem? Like a defendant with a family history of criminal activity? Anything like that?"

"No, Dad. Shoot, I only work little cases. I've never heard of someone killing a prosecuting attorney over traffic tickets."

"There's something you're overlooking."

"I don't think so," I said.

Dad spun his coffee cup in small circles with his thumbs. "Then it could be something you don't even know about yet."

"What do you mean?"

"I mean a case your office is getting ready to take. One you don't even know about yet." His spinning the cup in slow circles was driving me nuts. He kept his eyes on the cup while talking to me. "You're gonna need to figure it out. And fast. Have you contacted Daniel yet? Does he know you're ok?"

I lowered my voice to near a whisper, "I called him just before the guy started shooting at me. But I only left a message. In all the confusion, I dropped my phone in the wrecked car. I haven't tried to call him since."

Still spinning that damn cup, Dad said, "Good. Good. You'll have to tell me the exact details of everything on the ride home. It's best now for Daniel to not know anything, and maybe even better yet, to think you *are* dead." He took a long draw from his cup. "You ready?" he asked.

"Sure."

"Let's go," he said, backing his wheelchair from the table and spinning it to face the door.

I got up, walked behind his chair, and leaned over his shoulder, giving him a big hug. "Thanks, Dad," I told him in his ear. He patted my arms and when I squeezed him tightly, I felt the hidden holster under his left arm.

Growing up before his accident, I never really knew what my dad's job was. I once asked him and he only said that he worked in government relations. He didn't work regular weekdays like all of my friend's dads. He'd fly out on a plane for two or three days and then return for maybe a week, sometimes longer, before he'd fly out again.

I surveyed the parking lot as we made our way to his van. Sure enough, it was the same silver Odyssey I remembered.

Dad clicked the key fob and the sliding door opened. The thought went through my head to offer some assistance, but I knew better. I climbed into the passenger seat, bucked up and waited while Dad got situated.

He sang the phrase from the old Willie song sarcastically while turning the ignition key. "… on the road again."

I let out a deep sigh. Not an agitated sigh, a sigh of relief. I finally felt somewhat safe for the moment, but took another careful view of the parking lot as we began to roll out.

Letting my head lightly fall against the passenger side window, I said aloud, "Well, see ya later, Aspen. It's been nice." I closed my eyes and felt the road pass by under us.

I could feel the turns and the stops at each red light and I was starting to dose off when Dad slammed the brakes. "You fuck-head!" he yelled.

My eyes flashed open and I braced myself against the dash as the van's momentum came to a sudden standstill. I saw a bright red Charger stopped sideways in the road in front of us with his reverse lights on. Dad hit his fist against the horn, sounding off his frustration. "Must be a tourist. Idiot tried to make a quick U-turn in the middle of the road and that stupid car didn't turn sharp enough."

I laid my head against the window again and watched an arm poke out of the dark, tinted window and wave at us in an *I'm sorry* fashion. I closed my eyes and dozed off thinking about Daniel and the girls.

chapter eleven

The bright Florida sun beamed through the large glass windows making the white leather furniture glare as an overexposed image in the room. The old man wore a tan three-piece suit and sat like a statue on the left side of the couch with his elbow elevated on the white leather arm. He rested his chin in the palm of his hand, staring out to the ocean. In front of him, a fresh, uncut cigar lay on the coffee table. The gold lettering from the label on the cigar sparkled in the rays of sunlight shooting across the room.

The knock at the door was hardly loud enough to be heard. An almost submissive little knock, if one could be that.

"Come in," the old man said without turning to face the door.

"Señor Fuentes, Mister Mitchell wishes to see you," the assistant said.

The old man didn't move or turn. He kept his gaze to the ocean. "Let 'em in," he said. Behind him, he heard his assistant telling Mr. Mitchell in the other room that he may enter.

Footsteps made their way into the room. The door shut. A much younger and more casually-dressed fellow walked around the couch, stopping behind an armchair a few feet across and to the left of the old man. Wearing blue jeans and a tucked-in button-up shirt. He was tall. Not big, but muscular. The old man looked up to him, smiled, and motioned for him to sit. "Take a seat there. Get comfortable. I am so glad to finally meet you in person." He paused, studying his acquaintance.

"Nice to meet you too, Mr. Fuentes," the fellow said, leaning back in the white leather armchair and crossing one leg over the other at the knee with the posture of someone who was at ease with awkward meetings. Not submissive, but not overly aggressive either.

"Ah, call me Antonio," said the old man, leaning forward to get the cigar from the coffee table. "Antonio is fine." He sat back into the couch and flipped the cigar end over end with one hand. "Señor Jeff Mitchell …"

"Yes?"

"Señor Jeff Mitchell, would you like a cigar before we talk business?"

"No thanks."

Antonio smiled. "Do you smoke?"

Jeff gave one quick nod and said, "I do." He tapped his shirt chest pocket where an outline of a small box was visible. "Marlboro Reds. Good enough for me."

"Ah, but my cigars are not of the cheap dime-store variety. Do you know cigars, Señor Jeff?"

"Nope."

"These. These that I have," he said, still twirling and flipping the cigar, "... are the best money can buy. These are Cohiba cigars. Cohiba Behike cigars." He held the cigar motionless so that Jeff could see it clearly.

Jeff shifted in the chair. "Mr. Antonio, can we get to ..."

Antonio shook the cigar side to side at Jeff, "No, no, no. You came a long way, let's visit some first. Back to these cigars, each and every one of these has two holograms in the label. Do you know why, Señor Jeff?"

"No, I do not," Jeff said blandly.

"To prevent counterfeiting. Imagine a cigar being so valuable that people out there are willing to manufacture fakes."

Jeff relaxed.

Antonio continued, "In Cuba, I am from Cuba, you know. President Castro, himself, favored this brand." He held the cigar closer, observing the label. "A Cohiba Behike. Remember that, Señor Jeff. Remember that. So, how is the weather in New Jersey this time of year?"

"It's warm. Hot. A bit muggy," said Jeff. He'd let his attention go to the blue ocean view outside of the floor to ceiling windows. "This is a nice view you have here, Antonio."

Antonio nodded. "It is. It is."

Jeff's expression was one of someone who'd grown tired of bullshit talk. He faced Antonio. "I've been thinking about our last phone call. Do you really feel that an arrangement will be good for us? Both of us?"

Antonio set the cigar on the couch next to him and clasped his hands together in his lap, fingers intertwined. "Of course I do. We are businessmen, you and I. We are both successful in what we do, you and I. There should be no reason we cannot come to a peaceful arrangement of business territory."

Jeff sat forward with his elbows on his knees. His dark eyes focused on Antonio. "Have you begun?"

Antonio smiled, "I have. I have. Your technology resources have been very, very valuable."

chapter twelve

Dad nudged me in my side. "Hey, girl, wake up."

I stretched the best I could in the cramped quarters of the minivan's front seat. Thinking back, I had dozed off a few times during our trip. I remember talking about the girls when we were near Montrose, then chitchatting about useless stuff after Durango. Now, we'd apparently passed Farmington, New Mexico, and Dad had taken the last turn down his road.

The bright red numbers on the dash read 12:44. Just after midnight. Beyond the headlights of the van lay the black New Mexico night sky.

Looking through my window to the rear view mirror, I saw a trail of dust following us in the dim red glow from the brakes lights.

We slowed. The only sound was the *click-click* of the blinker. As the van turned right onto a rough dirt drive, there was a bright security light high on a pole ahead of us. It shone down through the blackness onto an old beat-up trailer house with the silhouette of car parked behind it. I'd never lived here at the trailer full-time, most of my nights were in the dorm on campus living the college life. I'd been back many times since, but driving up to it in the middle of *this* night was different. It appeared dark, and desolate, and lonely, and … sad.

The van came to a stop near the wheelchair ramp to the front door and a small cloud of dust floated by my window.

"Well, we're here," Dad said, turning off the engine. We both sat for a moment in silence. His time spent resting up a few seconds before the fight with his chair. And I, I watched the moths and other bugs flutter around the security light outside on that tall pole. It had been a long drive, the second in a day for him.

"Let's go get some rest," said Dad. "Your room is pretty much just as you left it. I'll hunt up some fresh sheets, though."

"You need any help getting in the house?" I asked, already knowing the answer.

"Nope." Dad unbuckled and turned in his seat. "But we need to look at that wound before you lay down. Make sure it's closing up good."

I stepped out, feeling the ever-so-slight chill of the desert night, and walked up the ramp to the front door, turning the knob and flipping on the lights for Dad. He never locked the door. Dad always said if you don't have anything worth stealing, there ain't no use in locking the door. He'd say the cost to replace the door from a break-in would outweigh the value of anything inside.

Still standing in the open doorway between the desert outside and the small cramped living room of the tiny mobile home, my eyes went to the darkened narrow hallway to my right. In that blackness, only the faint silver reflection from my room's doorknob could be seen.

The sound of my dad's wheelchair coming up the plywood deck on the ramp gave off eerie creaks from his weight. He was still a big man.

I made my way down the hall, reaching for the doorknob in the dark, and my mind brought me back in time. I was that young kid once again as I opened the door and turned the light on. The room was just as I'd left it. Just as he said.

The black curtains and black bedspread made me smile a little. Gothic culture and dress was the style of outcasts and … it was my style. Especially after Mom died. And for many, many years after, well into my twenties. The adult crowd used to think the black was for mourning, but it was really a way to push myself away from everyone. Black wasn't an inviting color and I felt much less approachable in black. I liked that. I'd never been one for useless conversation. Less so from people I didn't know.

"Get in here," Dad shouted. "Let me check that wound."

I turned off the light and met Dad in the living room. He was waiting for me with a flashlight, a bottle of peroxide, and a wooden stool placed in front of him. I knew not to argue, so I sat on the stool with my back to him. I lifted the Broncos shirt to expose my lower back, holding the extra fabric in a ball just under my breasts.

"Hmm," he said.

I twisted in an attempt to look back at him. "What do you mean with that *hmm* sound?"

"Keep straight and shush," he said, rubbing a finger across the entry wound, then tracing it across to the sewn up exit wound. "Did you see the gun?"

"No, Dad. Well, only from a distance briefly," I said. "I was kinda trying to not get shot. Why?"

"Nothing. Just figuring why they used such a small caliber pistol. That's all." I heard him open the peroxide bottle. "It wasn't a professional hit, and ... they're city thugs, like a gang or mafia-type, maybe dealing drugs, maybe dealing girls. Who knows."

"How can you tell?"

"Tell what?" he asked.

"Both," I replied. "The small caliber and the kind of criminal they are?"

He touched the entry wound and said, "Entry wounds are hard to tell sometimes, but the exit wound," he paused, "... the exit wound here is rather small and there's not a lot of damage on the exit even though the bullet only went through soft tissue. A small caliber will lose a lot of momentum, even in the soft tissue. If this would'a been a nine or a forty caliber, then we would have a much uglier exit." I felt the cold liquid as he dabbed the wound with a cotton ball of peroxide. "Come on, Kait, you should know this stuff with all those marksmanship trophies you got."

"Yeah right," I replied. "Ok, what about them being city thugs?"

"Goes back to the weapon of choice. The small pistol. Three-eighties, twenty-twos and the like, are cheap, small, easily hidden, and most of all, they're disposable." He capped the bottle and leaned back in his wheelchair. "You're all good. Go get some rest. We'll start fresh tomorrow."

Morning came early, bright, and with new level of soreness. Not outright pain, just soreness. The smell of coffee, eggs, and toast had made their way into my room even with the closed door. Sunlight peeked through the sides of the thick black curtain.

Swinging my legs over the bed and sitting upright, I lifted my arms and stretched as high as I could. It was the first time I'd been able to move like this in two days. Dad banged and clanged in the kitchen, fussing some in between.

I sat there looking around the room. The walls were a white-ish color behind all the dark decorations. As an adult, I could see this as a depressing setting. Aside from the black curtain and bedspread, the only two pieces of furniture in the room were also black. A dresser and a nightstand. I can still remember hauling them outside at the Phoenix house by myself one weekend with some cans of spray paint. I'd had Dad buy the cans for me, but he didn't know why. When he saw what I did, he was pissed. Then, I was pissed. We both eventually got over it. That was the year after Mom …

To the far wall next to the closet were some cheap shelves screwed to the paneling, black of course. The shelves were adorned with trophies and ribbons. On some small nails lining the edge of the lower shelf hung ribbons of all colors and designs. I stood up, went to the shelf and fingered through them. All martial arts awards and two marksmanship ones. The metal pendants that weighed each of them down were embossed with images of a long chapter in my life. Most of them from various traditional tournaments based upon weight class, age, and belt rank.

Mixed in, were a few from private tournaments that incorporated the weapons training that Mom was insistent on, such as the staff, short stick, and cane. I pulled one out from behind the others and held the heavy brass pendant in the palm of my hand. I was awarded this one for use of the Sai, a long, dull dagger about twenty inches in length with two metal protrusions that served as side guards. Mom told me to learn the Sai well, that if I'd learn the techniques, then I could substitute the Sai with a pocket knife, a stick found on the ground, and even a car key. I gripped the pendant tightly. That tournament was my last. Mom drove me the three hours there, cheered me on, and brought me to Pizza Hut after. It was the day after my thirteenth birthday. She was gunned down the next day in a robbery-gone-wrong inside of a little convenience store only five blocks from our house in Phoenix. I watched it all happen from the passenger seat of her car.

I let the medal drop from my hand and it swung back behind the others, out of sight. My attention went to the trophies so carefully lined up on the two shelves. Dad was a gun guy. He'd always been. And he loved it each time I did well with a firearm. I scanned the engraved brass plaques.

The first one from the left read -*Precision Pistol .45 Caliber*-.

Then -*Precision Pistol .22 Caliber Rapid Fire*-. There were three of those from different years.

Two more labeled -*Precision Pistol .22 Caliber Timed Fire*-.

One -*Mid-Range Rifle 500 Yards, Scope*-. I remembered that one well.

Two -*Mid-Range Rifle 600 Yards, Iron Sights*-. I still say those were just luck.

Two -*Intercollegiate Sports Pistol Individual Class*-.

One -*Intercollegiate Rapid Fire Pistol*-.

And the last five were from various years, but all read -.*45 Caliber National Match Course*-.

I competed with firearms well into my junior year of college. It was about then that I decided I needed to focus more on what would actually get me a job after graduation. A smart decision and probably for the best. I also met Daniel around that time.

"Hey, girl, I've got breakfast in here," Dad said from the kitchen.

Dad was sliding eggs from a pan onto two plates when I entered. The kitchen counter was in direct view from my hallway and across the living room. It was u-shaped with a five-foot-long counter blocking the space off and giving some dimension to it. A nice kitchen it was not. Even for an old beater of a trailer house, it was an ugly kitchen. Right after Dad bought the place, he and one of his friends tore out the original counter and cabinets since he was wheelchair bound. They rebuilt the entire kitchen much lower so Dad could live in there as normal as possible. The sink, stove, and counters, they were all lowered. They even moved the upper cabinets down. Dad still couldn't really reach them since he couldn't tip-toe or anything, but he'd always used one of those extendable clamp grabber things for the stuff up there.

Some parts, like the counter top, they could re-use. But what they had to build from scratch, they did so with the cheapest plywood they could get their hands on.

Dad never got around to painting that plywood.

It was an ugly kitchen.

It didn't matter much to Dad, though. Mom was gone and so was I, mostly. I was in my Sophomore year of college when the explosion injured him. A gas leak in our old house in Phoenix. Blew up the entire master bedroom and kitchen. I'd heard news stories about how gas leaks can cause explosions, but I'd never given it any afterthought.

Dad chose to get treatment out east, then used some saved up cash to buy the place, twenty acres of New Mexico desert dirt with an old abandoned trailer house on it. He had made sure to have my room set up just as it was in our Phoenix house. Even though I only came home on weekends and holidays, he was determined to have it perfect for me.

I sat at the small round table in the only chair and waited with a smile. I knew he would want to serve me. He liked being a daddy. He really did.

"I hope you like it," he said. "I haven't cooked for anyone in a long time. Well, I did cook some burgers for that kid I hired a few months ago to help with the old car. Anyway, I'm no professional chef."

"It's great, Dad. It's simply wonderful. Thanks."

He locked his wheelchair in place at his side of the table. His spot was well-worn. The table's cheap veneer and imitation woodgrain had been rubbed off to a dull white color where his elbows regularly rested.

He took a bite from the fork loaded with eggs and asked, "So, did you figure out who did this to you yet?"

The tone of his conversation was so plain considering the subject. Like it was normal breakfast conversation. "Well?" he sounded when I didn't give an answer.

"No, Dad. I have no idea."

"It's gotta be something with your job," he said.

"Dad, it doesn't make sense. I work with petty cases. It just doesn't make any sense."

He took another bite. "It's the only thing that does make sense. Unless you're into some bad shit on your own." He looked me in the eye. "Are you?"

"Am I what?"

"Are you involved with something? Drugs, money laundering, selling information?"

"No, Dad. I'm not."

Dad's attention went back to his plate. He mumbled, "Can't be Daniel."

"What do you mean by that?" I asked.

"Oh, I just mean that I doubt *he* hired a hit or anything. Are you two getting along?"

A thought like that would have never crossed my mind. "Yes, we are doing fine." I stopped and thought for a second, then asked, "What about when you said you doubt he would have hired a hit?"

"He's a dork. That's why."

"He is not," I answered back with the voice of a little girl.

Dad smiled, laughed, and said, "Yeah, he's a dork. I love him, but yeah, he's a dork. Back to all seriousness, you really need to figure it out. Who. Not just who those two guys in Aspen were, but who hired them."

"And then what? That's where I'm lost." The lightheartedness faded away and reality set in. "The only thing I know is that they were able to track me and find me all too easily."

Dad clicked his fork against his plate with an annoying sound. He was staring at me with no expression.

"Ok, Dad, let's say I do figure out who wants me dead, then what? What do I do then?"

Dad's answer was short and to the point. "Kill 'em."

My mouth dropped open. "Kill them? It's that simple? I just kill them?"

"Yup," he said with his last bite. "Killing them is simple. Getting into position to kill them and then getting away is the hard part. The killing part is easy."

I'd never heard him talk like that. I honestly didn't know where it was coming from. He was just a guy who went around the country handling business meetings.

He'd already had both elbows on the tabletop and he let both arms fall to the table with a *thud,* landing on each side of his empty plate. "Look, Kait, when someone wants you dead, they *will* succeed unless you get them first. If you go to the cops, then you draw a lot of unwanted attention and if they can't get to you because of that, they'll get to the ones you love the most." His eyes went down to the table. "When you're the one left living, they've still killed you. They've killed you inside and … that can be much worse." A small glitter of wetness formed in the corner of his eye.

My emotions jumped at his statement. "Mom? Did those robbers intend to kill her?" I asked. "Was there more to it? Dad?"

He didn't reply. He didn't move or offer any reaction to my questions for what seemed like minutes. Unlocking his chair, he rolled it away from the table in one quick motion, grabbed his plate, and headed to the sink.

"Dad, you didn't answer me," I said in a commanding tone, but it did no good.

He spun his chair to face me and changed the subject. "We need you to brush up on your skills and …"

"Skills, what skills?"

"Marksmanship, martial arts. Those skills."

I pushed my chair back and stood up. "I'm no master at any of those. Sure, I was good in the fighting tournaments and shooting sports, but … I've never actually injured anyone. I've never shot anyone. I don't know if I could do it."

He waved his hand in the air like he was swatting my arguments away and rolled to the fridge, pulled out a Coke, and cracked it open. "Ok, once you find out who ordered your hit, you can do with that information what you want. Go to the police and have them arrested. Whatever. Fine. But you have guys looking for you right now. You're gonna need to be ready for anything in your search for intel. Even if you don't wanna kill the main sonuvabitch, you'll need to protect yourself because he, she, whoever, still wants *you* dead and they'll still have their guys out hunting for you."

"No, Dad. Just no," I argued.

"If not, then what? You can't hide out here forever. Well, you could. But we'd drive each other nuts."

I rubbed my forehead hard and scratched into my scalp with my fingers. "I need to go think. I'll be back." I walked through the door outside onto the wooden ramp.

chapter thirteen

It was early and the desert air was still cool. Mornings out here really were beautiful. I paced back and forth on the small landing of the ramp with my arms crossed. How could Dad so calmly suggest killing someone? What was he not telling me about Mom? As I paced, I remembered her. The way she talked. The way she tilted her head when she smiled.

And Dad. That bit about *the killing is the easy part*. How would he know? Had he ever killed anyone? I was gonna ask when I went back in.

The most important thing was to figure out who didn't want me around anymore. And why. If Dad was right, then I needed access to our files at work … in North Carolina. I needed to get to the East Coast and I needed to get there without those two guys correcting their first mistake beforehand.

For the next five minutes, I continued to pace. I knew Dad could hear the back and forth thumps on the wooden planks. He'd probably say I was pouting.

Those two guys found me once and they'd find me again as soon as I stepped back out into civilization.

Unless.

I needed to be … someone else.

Daniel and the girls were probably safe as long as I was invisible. Whoever had been watching me was likely also watching my family waiting, waiting for me to reappear.

I could do it. I could. All I needed to do was keep myself alive until I could get into my office.

I could defend myself.

If I were attacked again.

Maybe.

I didn't do a very good job on that mountain in Aspen, but at that time, I didn't know what I was to them. I didn't know that I was … prey. I was being hunted and stalked like prey. That thought alone made my blood boil.

Storming back inside, slamming the flimsy door closed behind me, I went right up to Dad who had his wheelchair next to the kitchen table sipping on his Coke.

"You get your brain workin' now?" he asked.

I stood directly in front of him with my hands on my hips, the right of which felt sore under the pressure of my hand, but I didn't care. "Have you ever killed anyone?"

He set his Coke down on the table surface and responded with a shrug of his shoulders, "Does it matter?"

"Yes. It does. It does matter."

He reached behind him and rubbed the back of his neck. "A few."

"What do you mean 'a few'?" I asked without budging.

"Like I said. A few." The close space of me standing over him had been too much and he rolled back a couple feet so he wouldn't have to tilt his head up too awkwardly. "Kait, I had an odd job when you were a kid. And yes, I had to take care of some business every now and then."

"How many?"

"Oh hell, I don't know. Let's not get into it, ok? That was a long time ago." He took a deep breath and stared into my eyes with an uncomfortable silence before saying, "We have to focus on getting you set up for some practice shooting."

Not completely satisfied with the lack of an answer and knowing I wasn't going to get any further with him, I let my tension fade away and relaxed. "I don't have my target pistols anymore. Remember, we sold them to pay for college books?"

"Those guns wouldn't be any good anyway. Can you do me a favor?"

"Yes," I answered.

"Go into my room and on the middle closet shelf is a toolbox. Bring me a phillips-head screwdriver, please."

Confused by the off-the-wall request, I told him that I would.

"Here," I said upon my return, "one phillips-head screwdriver."

He rolled his chair to the section of the counter that protruded out to form the u-shape of the kitchen, leaned way forward in his chair and pointed to a screw underneath the overhanging lip.

I squatted to follow his point. Turning my head, I could see it. A black sheetrock screw head.

"You go around on all three sides and unscrew each one of those," said Dad.

As in most kitchens I'd been in, the countertop overlapped the cabinet frame by a few inches. On my knees, I made my way around the three sides of the counter, fumbling with the screwdriver until all ten screws were out. I stood up with a moan and a handful of black one-inch long screws.

Dad wheeled to the very end of the counter saying, "Set those screws down on the table or somewhere. We'll need to put them back in a minute. Get over there," he said, pointing to the other end. There was a very nice seam where one part of the countertop joined up with the rest. "Lift up," he ordered. "Lift, and tilt it over onto the floor. Careful now. Don't fuck up my fancy kitchen counter."

As we lifted and tilted the countertop over, my entire childhood came into focus. The martial arts training, the shooting classes, Dad's friends with weird names, the late night visits by doctors, those urgent phone calls making Dad drive out for work, all of it.

Just under the countertop was a false bottom only six inches deep. The main cabinet still possessed normal drawers and storage. But there was the shallow, hidden cavity between the drawers and the countertop that was so perfectly constructed, no one would have ever known. I know I'd never noticed.

A fine black padded-velvet lining trimmed out the cavity and inside, carefully placed and arranged on the velvet, were weapons I'd never seen before. Nothing like the hunting rifles or target pistols I'd grown up with. These were specialized weapons.

Perfect.

Flawless.

Spotless.

Dark … and deadly.

Situated inside were six different types of pistols. Three with long silencers attached to the end of the barrels. One with a flashlight. And another with a scope.

Then, there were the rifles. Two of them. One really petite and short in length. A tiny barrel diameter and an almost fragile-in-appearance black plastic stock. The other was much more formidable. It was long and heavy-looking with a huge scope on it. The scope itself was at least two feet long. It even had a small fold-out stand attached under the stock's front end.

The only thing I could get out of my mouth was a mix between a statement and a question. "Dad, what is this?"

"These are finely-tuned instruments," he said, looking over them like long-lost friends he hadn't seen in quite some time.

It was a sight to behold.

Dad carefully picked up a very tiny black and silver pistol along with its clip holster and handed it to me saying, "Lay this one on the table." He then studied between two other handguns. Both of them long with silencers attached. Picking one up, he held it in position, sighting down the barrel toward my room. He'd relax, then raise it quickly again with arms outstretched a few times. Going through the motions of firing. Repeating this with the other similar pistol, he finally handed me his second pick.

When I took hold of it, the weight surprised me. Hefty, but manageable. It was well over a foot long in total with the pistol and silencer together. All black without a single hint of silver anywhere on it. It was blocky and basic-looking in shape, similar to so many other military handguns. But it felt so perfect and balanced.

Dad watched me observe it before saying, "Overall length is fifteen inches. Nine-millimeter Sig Sauer P226

SAO. One of the most accurate nine-mils made. Paired with that sound suppressor and some subsonic one hundred-forty grain weight ammo, firing that handgun will only sound like a light car door closing." He sat back in his chair, crossing his arms and watching me. "If the wind is right, and a few birds are chirping in the trees, no one will ever hear a thing."

I set it down on the kitchen table and picked up the much smaller one. It literally fit in the palm of my hand and weighed nothing. The top metal portion with the barrel was a matte silver while the lower grip and trigger areas were a flat black composite material.

"That one," said Dad. "It's for close-range work. A Beretta Pico, if I remember the name right. Smaller caliber, it's a three-eighty with a six-round capacity. Nice and effective. Accurate, not so much because it's such a tiny pistol with a short barrel." He let me study the weapon a moment, then added, "Oh, and never load the clips or handle the brass casings with your bare fingers. Use gloves, thick paper napkins, or something like that."

"Don't touch the shells?" I asked.

"No. Fingerprints. We don't want fingerprints on anything that might get left behind." Dad backed up his chair to the countertop where we had set it and ordered, "Come on, let's get this top back on and screwed down again."

chapter fourteen

The ring of his cell phone pulled Daniel from a deep sleep. He'd overslept. The motel clock near the TV read 10:05am. He reached over, grabbed his cell phone and held it inches from his eyes so that he could read the incoming caller. His glasses still on the side table.

In blurry lettering on the screen amid the ringing, he saw, Aspen Police Dept. "Yes, hello. This is Daniel."

"Mr. Cline," the familiar voice of Officer Cantrell said.

Daniel sat up in the bed. "Yes. Anything?"

"Mr. Cline, I wanted to let you know that we have filed the formal missing person's report."

"Ok, thank you," he blankly replied. "Now what?"

"We'll keep our eyes open."

"That's it? No more searching?" Daniel's voice rose with each syllable as he was unable to hide his frustration. "You're done?"

"Mr. Cline, we have interviewed every homeowner within five miles of your wife's accident. We have contacted and left pictures with every ER doctor and also sent out alerts to local businesses." Officer Cantrell kept her dialog professional and lacking of emotion. "We've had a team of search and rescue volunteers go out to the site, fanning their efforts for many miles of mountain terrain. They've come up with nothing. No sign of Kaitlyn."

Daniel swung his legs over the side of the bed, slipping on his hiking shoes still covered in dust and caked-on mountain-stream mud.

"Mr. Cline, at this point, all we can do is get the missing persons report out there. I have already sent it to other agencies throughout the state and also contacted the FBI. I've not heard anything back from them yet."

"Alright."

"Mr. Cline, you should return home to your daughters. They need you and I assure you that I will contact you immediately with any news."

He rubbed his head and told her, "Ok, thanks."

He'd decided late last night that his own personal search was going to continue. Having purchased a terrain map from the local outdoor store the night before, he'd drawn a grid pattern over the area of the accident and marked off those more populated grids where he guessed the search and rescue crews had already been. There were lots of nooks and crannies hidden within the small valleys and gorges. Places people never looked for or noticed. He had to search those. Kaitlyn could have taken shelter in the wild somewhere. She could be hurt and waiting. She could have exhausted her lungs yelling for help. She could be in need of water. She could be dying somewhere, out there, in those mountains.

The girls were fine with Daniel's mom until he returned ... returned with Kaitlyn. Olivia and Mattie still didn't know. His last phone call before he flew out of North Carolina raised suspicion with the girls, but Daniel blew it off, still confirming to them that their mom was ok, just held up or something in Colorado. If he went back without her, though, it would simply break the girls. The truth would be too hard to say. Hell, it was hard to admit to himself.

Still sitting at the edge of the bed with his phone, he went to his voice messages and played Kaitlyn's last message again. Closing his eyes, he listened to her voice. "Dan..., I've been ... a wreck. I'm hurt, but ... bad. I love you. Tell ... girls I love them. I'll be ... I need to go now ... I love you. I love you."

chapter fifteen

Four days of handgun shooting drills with evening trips to a private martial arts teacher had worn my muscles down past fatigue. Being an assistant attorney was not a very physically-demanding occupation, so my body was not prepared for such activity. Nor was it prepared to be rolled down a mountain and shot in the back exactly one week earlier.

One week.

I sat up in the gothic bed of my childhood years, cross-legged, and rubbed my eyes. What a change my life had taken is such a short time. I needed to get this all resolved quickly before Daniel and the girls lost any hope that I was alive. Shit, I wished I could just let them know somehow.

The sound of a car door shutting outside startled me. I jumped up and parted the black curtain only enough to see Dad's wheelchair closing the gap between the van and the wooden ramp with a plastic sack in his lap.

Rushing through my room, I ran to the front door to open it for him. I did it more out of human nature to help a person in need on my part than because he actually needed the help.

"G'morning, girl," he said, wheeling right past me. "Go get dressed and look alive. I might cook up some breakfast." Once in the living room, he spun around and looked me up and down. I was in some old pajamas that I used to wear sixteen years ago.

Shaking his head, he grinned. An honest grin. It was a happy face that I had not seen in a really long time.

I stood there just staring at him.

He broke my awkward glance by saying, "Just joking. You look good. Now, go wake up. I'll get started."

We ate without much conversation. I was starving and we had pretty much run out of topics to talk about over the last few days. This week was the most time I'd spent with him since he moved out here after healing up.

The plastic sack he'd carried in earlier lay in crumpled pile on the counter. I studied it after finishing my breakfast, but didn't dare ask. It was the only thing he must have gone to town for. There was an obvious shape to it, a box of some sort inside the loose bag. One corner of it formed a sharp point against the white plastic.

Dad saw me looking at it. "Here," he said. "Take our plates to the sink for me and bring back that sack."

I returned, setting the sack in front of him and sat back down in my chair.

With one hand, he slid it across to me. "It's prepaid for at least a couple months, anonymous, and untraceable back to you as your real name."

Opening the white plastic sack, I pulled out a cell phone box. It was nothing special, but what was odd was that I'd lost my phone a week ago and hadn't missed it at all.

Dad made a slap noise against the tabletop to get my attention and pointed to me with a stern finger. "Now, you cannot call Daniel. You hear me? You risk your family's lives if you do."

I nodded.

"I'm serious. The time will come, but right now they can't know you're alive." He wheeled backwards from the table and turned to the sink to begin washing the plates.

I had to speak up over the sound of the water. "If I can't call anyone, what do I need a phone for?"

He was quickly scrubbing with his back to me and answered loudly, "You'll need it. For directions. For taking photos of any of those documents you might find at your office. For making any hotel or flight reservations. And for calling me. I'm gonna need to know that you're safe." Tuning off the faucet, he spun around and came back to the table.

My eyes met his and I simply didn't have any words. This all still didn't seem real.

He locked his chair and laid his arms on the tabletop. "You're ready enough and healed up enough to get things going now."

I straightened my spine and pulled my shoulders back. "Dad, I ... I don't know."

"Ah bullshit, don't undersell yourself. You are damn good with a gun. Way better than any run-of-the-mill cop or criminal. And you already know that you can hold your own in hand-to-hand combat. Besides, you're my daughter. My blood. Like I kept telling you all week, just slow your brain down, think, and plan ahead."

"But ..."

He held the palm of his hand up. "Like you yourself said, all you need to do is get to the office and figure out who has any reason to be after you. This week's training was for you to be ready in case you have to defend yourself. Hopefully, you won't need to."

I could hear that damned tone in his voice. I leaned forward and said, "You know I'm going to have to use those pistols. You know it, don't you? You don't think I'll get all the way to North Carolina and figure this out without those men finding me, do you?"

He only shook his head side to side slowly as his way of saying *no*.

"How do you? Huh, how do you know?"

"Experience," he said. "Experience."

I reached up with the palm of my hand and rubbed my forehead. "Shit, just shit."

"Calm down, come back to reality," said Dad. "You'll have to go to San Diego first."

"Huh?"

"Yeah, you'll meet a guy in San Diego at an office building. There, he can turn you into someone else. New name, new hometown, new driver's license, and credit card. An alias will help you travel undetected." He reached into his shirt pocket and pulled out a key and a small bundle of cash. Setting them on the table, he told me, "Here's the key to your mom's old car. It runs. And enough cash to get you to California and a couple hotel rooms."

"So," I asked, "what do I tell this guy? Does he know I'm coming? Do you know him?"

Dad gazed off to the ceiling. I could tell he was thinking of how to either lie to me or tell me only what I needed to know. He said, "No, he doesn't know that you're coming. He doesn't even know you exist. He doesn't know that I still exist." Dad took in a deep breath. "Yeah, I know him. He was my handler. He assigned me to various cases, issues that needed to be taken care of … in a quick and permanent manner."

Dad was definitely picking his words carefully.

"His name is Elmore Williams. He's still there, hasn't retired yet. Probably due to retire very soon, though."

Confused, I asked, "He thinks you're dead? How?"

Dad shifted in his chair. "Well, Mom wasn't here anymore and I was tired of the job. A few weeks before the natural gas explosion at our old house in Phoenix, I took in this homeless guy I met in town one night. He seemed a good guy. About my age. Not a drunk, not on drugs. Just said his life went downhill." Shrugging his shoulders, Dad continued. "I was in the bedroom at the moment of the explosion and he was in the kitchen near the stove and fridge. I saw his body when the medics hauled me out on the stretcher. Shit, his head was gone. Like completely gone. Anyway, to make a long story short, I'm pretty sure the explosion wasn't an accident. The Phoenix newspaper said that one man was killed in it with no mention of another wounded. So, after rehab, which I was able to get done under a fake name using cash, I had a buddy go back to the house with a moving van and a car dolly. He loaded up most of the furniture, my things, all your stuff, your mom's car, and that homeless guy's ID. Then I became him, the homeless guy, as far as the rest of this world is concerned." He grinned at the look of disbelief on my face. "You wouldn't have known. It's been an easy-to-hide detail due to the fact that you only call me 'Dad,' I pay cash in public, and I make sure to never give out my name to anyone when I'm with you and your family."

Unbelievable. I shook off that last bit of newly-acquired information and asked, "What do I tell this Elmore fellow when I meet him?" This was a lot for me to take in.

"Tell him ..." Dad paused. "Tell him that you're my daughter. Use my name, the one you know. Tell him that in some papers you were given after my death, there were instructions to go to him if you were ever in need of help."

"Do you trust him?" I asked.

"Yeah, I trust him. I don't want him to know that I'm alive. But yes, I trust him to help you if you ask for it. He owes me."

chapter sixteen

Mom's old Toyota Camry carried me to California with ease given the fact that it had been parked behind Dad's trailer house for the last sixteen years. It was dark blue with window tint that had begun to bubble. A four-door model with a cracked taillight and glazed over headlights. It had seen its better years.

  Before I drove out in the night, Dad told me to sell it if I needed to. I agreed, but deep down I knew that would be a hard thing to do. Mom had driven me back and forth from school every day and to all my practices and taekwondo classes in it. I'd spent so many miles in the passenger seat staring out of the window. The last time I heard her laugh or saw her amazingly beautiful smile was in this car.

  It may have been my imagination, but I swear the driver's seat was still formed to Mom's frame and weight. It seemed to fit me all too perfectly and I wondered how similar I was to her in size. The leather steering wheel had peeled near the bottom where Mom tended to always hold it. It was like an imprint from her hand and holding that part of the wheel made me feel as if I were touching her. Yeah, the car would be very hard to sell to some shitty shyster in a discount suit running a used car-lot.

    I pulled into the parking lot as the clock on the dash clicked over to 8:23am. It had been a long night driving without stopping to rest. But I wasn't tired. The nervousness and anticipation of the unknown surrounding this Elmore guy kept me awake. Thankfully, the trip was an uneventful one since I was under strict orders from Dad to not share my identity with anyone. I'd hidden my ID and credit cards under the seat with the three-eighty, but I had no idea of what to say if I were stopped or questioned by any authority figure.

    Turning the car off, I sat there with my eyes on the tall building of marble with glass windows. It was well-kept and busy. Nicely landscaped and it carried the appearance of a reputable office complex. After parking, I'd watched at least fifteen people enter, give or take. I could see a plaque next to the entrance door, but couldn't make out any of the wording. Obviously though, there were quite a few different offices or companies inside.

    Reaching over, I slid my hand under the passenger seat to retrieve the little three-eighty caliber. The nine-millimeter Sig with the silencer was well hidden inside one of the rear seat cushions through an opening I'd cut from underneath. Carefully, I worked the three-eighty's holster between my skin and jeans, directly in the middle of my back, low and in the small arch where it wouldn't create a bulge or give off any sign of its presence under my shirt. The clip of the holster securely latched onto my belt.

Here goes nothing, I thought.

On my walk toward the large glass entrance door, I trembled and my heart pounded. I was literally scared. If the meeting didn't go as Dad hoped, then what? I'd be stuck here in California with no plan. I stopped at the door, rubbed my hand against the thigh of my jeans to get the sweat off, and pulled the door open.

"Good morning, do you have an appointment with one of our offices today?" the sweet little college girl asked from behind a concrete counter only ten feet from the entrance.

"No, I don't," I said, reading the office list posted behind her, searching for the name of Elmore Williams.

Still with a smile, she gave me her rehearsed speech. "I'm sorry, but all companies represented here require an appointment. Would you like for me to set up an appointment for you? Who are you here to see?"

Not seeing his name anywhere on the list, I told her, "I need to see Elmore Williams. I need to see him as soon as possible." I let my eyes finally meet hers without a blink, a smile, or any emotion.

I watched the smile drop from her face. She picked up the phone receiver and dialed in a couple numbers.

"Yes, this is Carla at reception. I have someone here to see Mr. Williams." She then covered the phone with her hand and asked me, "Could you tell me your name, please?"

"No," I answered.

"Who shall I say is here to see Mr. Williams?"

I leaned over the counter to get closer and said in a monotone voice, "Tell him that I'm the daughter of an old acquaintance."

She said back into the phone, "This person will only tell me that she is the daughter of an acquaintance of Mr. Williams." The girl said *yes* and *ok* a couple times and hung up. "Miss, you can take the elevator up to the ninth floor and go to office 925."

I glanced up to the list on the wall. There was no 925 listed. "Thanks," I said and walked to the stainless steel box inset into the wall. I appeared calm and collected, but my finger quivered as it pressed the button.

The numbers in an elevator can feel like a never-ending torture. At the final landing, the digital readout said 9 and doors took the long two-seconds to finally open. The sign on the wall in front of me showed a left arrow for offices 900 - 912 and a right arrow for offices 913 - 924.

To the right it is. As I walked down the wide, carpeted, and brightly-lit hallway, each door had its own glass window and logo for whatever business was behind it. I passed an insurance office, a real estate office, two attorneys, and then I quit looking at them. I could see it ahead. The door at the end of the hall had no glass window. Just a plain, tan-painted metal door with the numbers 925 on it.

I didn't knock. The door handle was smooth and quiet under the pressure as it unlatched. Standing there, I lightly pushed the door open and let it swing freely. Slowly.

From a single desk to the left inside the room, a petite lady about my own age with long red hair and pale skin greeted me. "Come on in and please shut the door behind you. You wish to see Mr. Williams?"

"Yes," I said, pushing the door shut behind my back with the tips of my fingers.

"He will see you now. You can go on in," she said, gesturing to a set of tinted solid glass french doors in the middle of the long wall across the room. The tint was dark enough to only allow a few obscure shapes to be seen through them. There were no door handles, just brass push plates on each door where they met in the middle.

"Ok," I said nervously. Approaching the doors closer, the silhouette of a desk and a person sitting behind it began to come into focus.

With a nervous hand on each brass plate, I pushed both doors open simultaneously. Behind the desk, a large man sat looking very ... well, very pleasant and inviting. His skin nearly matched the dark brown leather chair and his hair was a consistent shade of silver. The office was formal, and minimal. A large window behind him overlooked the city. His simple, casual checkered shirt didn't fit in.

Waving his hand, he eagerly told me, "Come in, come in. Have a seat."

Steadily, I walked up to the front of the desk and stood, deciding to stand rather than sit in the chair to my right. I heard the doors behind me settling into their closed position.

He leaned back in the leather chair clasping his hands together over his midsection. The chair bounced slightly from what must have been a rocking pressure from his feet. "What can I help you with? You surely didn't find me by mischance. Introduce yourself."

Leaning forward only slightly, I set both hands onto the surface of his desk and said, "My father left some instructions for me in documents to be opened after his death."

"Yes?" he asked, consistently rocking that chair.

"His instructions said that if I ever needed anything or was in trouble, to contact you." I carefully watched his face for any expression that would give me worry. There was none. The smile on his face and twinkle in his eye seemed genuine.

He asked, "Now tell me, who was your father who left this note for you?"

"Chris — Falcon," I let the name leave my lips slowly. "Chris Falcon," I repeated.

His rocking motion came to a stop and he tilted his head sideways. "Ah, Miss Falcon. Your father was a good man. Such a shame to have lost him to a crazy accident." Mr. Williams closed his eyes as if bringing up long, forgotten memories. "Yes, Miss Falcon. May I call you Miss Falcon?"

"Kait, you can call me Kait," I answered.

"Kait, I held and still have a great deal of respect for your father. He was an amazing team member, as was your mother. What is it that I can do for you?"

My mind shut down altogether for a second. My mother? I shook it off and continued, "Mr. Williams, I need to become someone else for a short time so that I can travel back east to retrieve some documents. I need to be untraceable and un-trackable."

"Are you in trouble? Have you committed a crime?" he asked.

"I did not commit a crime. But trouble *is* following me." I stopped talking a moment to think and decide how much information I should share. "Two men attempted to kill me a week ago. They used a pickup to force my car off of a Colorado mountain road and shot me in the back. I need to get to my office in North Carolina and go through some files with the hopes of figuring out who hired those two."

"Then?"

"Then get that info to the authorities so I can return to my normal life." I straightened up and crossed my arms. "That's the plan anyway."

With a squeak from the chair, he leaned forward, placing his elbows on the desk surface. "Normal life? Do you have a family, Kait?"

I shook my head, "No."

He stood up from his chair and put his hands in the pockets of his slacks. Relaxed and tall. He was a statue of a man, with a commanding and even dominant air about him. "Tell you what. I'll venture a bet that there is a lot more to this story that you're not telling me. I'm sure you're leaving a few details out since you came to me and not the police. But I'm not going to dig. For your father, I'll help you."

I was at a loss for words. Not knowing where the conversation should go next, I remained silent, waiting for more from him.

He stepped out from behind the desk and began to pace in a large circle around the desk and then behind me.

I stayed put, listening to his footsteps.

"Obviously, there's some urgency in your request Kait. So ..." His path led him around behind his desk again. I felt much better with him in front of me. "My assistant, Monica, will work on your new name, birth certificate, and social security number. And I'll get you a credit card." He saw the quick raise of my eyebrows and said, "No worries about the money. Just be as frugal as possible and I'll handle paying for your expenses until you get this issue of yours resolved."

The tension was gradually leaving my body and I let my arms fall to my side. My thumbs latching loosely into the corners of my jean pockets.

Sitting back down in his chair, he said, "I can have you ready to go by tomorrow night. Will that work?"

"It'll have to," I replied.

"You'll need to get some clothes that you'd normally not wear. A complete change of style. Cut your hair, maybe dye it. You need to look … well, not like you. Get that done today, then tomorrow morning we'll take a picture of the new you for your ID."

Honestly not knowing how to reply, I simply said, "Thank you, Mr. Williams."

"Call me Elmore. I'll see you in the morning after you get some rest."

I turned and walked toward the glass doors.

"Oh," he said, "there'll be no need to check in with the receptionist in the lower lobby. Just come on up. She won't question you."

chapter seventeen

Pulling the phone out of my pocket as I crossed the concrete parking lot, I opened the car door and slid into the driver's seat. I left the door open and scrolled to the maps application on my phone. Service was slow and I leaned back in the seat, resting my head against the headrest.

I had two stops before finding a motel room for the night, a drug store, and second-hand clothes shop. Elmore was right, if I was going to be someone else, I needed to truly look like someone else.

I studied the office building, scanning the height of it. It was a tall building, more than nine floors. My eyes detected something. I hadn't been looking for anything particular aside from basic observation. But it stood out. A shadow. A shadow in one of the windows. I sat forward and focused through my windshield. Counting glass windows from the base of the building up, I came to nine where the shadow stood. It was him. Elmore was standing there watching me. Watching me through the big glass window of his office. Slamming the car door shut, I sat back and twisted the ignition key.

Only a few blocks away was a *Mom and Pop* drug store. I guessed it was a *Mom and Pop* by the name, Clovis's Medicine Chest, not a franchise name.

An old little lady with an even more aged posture asked me if I needed help. I answered with a question. "Where's the hair color ... and scissors?"

"Oh, follow me. I'll show you?" she said, walking away at a pace faster than I expected her to. Coming to sudden stop, she pointed to a small row of boxes. "What color are you after? Your hair is so pretty now."

"I need black. Just black."

She furrowed her brow and reached for a box of black and handed it to me. "Let's go get those shears and ... is there anything else?" She led the way down the aisle.

"Yes, could you point me to a used clothing store?"

Still walking, she said without looking back, "I can. I'll give you directions at the counter."

Her directions were good, very good. She and her husband knew the neighborhood well. They'd owned and operated that store for thirty-three years. That was her story anyway. She was a sweet lady and a natural-born talker.

Only minutes away, I found it with the old lady's overly-detailed map points and compass directions. Three rolling racks of shirts outside of the front door eliminated the need for the worn-out signage on the brick wall. I was still using up the small amount of cash Dad had given me, but the bundle had decreased in size. It's thickness had dwindled at each gas station driving through the night.

The store was well-marked and I headed to the women's pants. Black. I wanted black, gothic black, and I needed a pair baggy enough in the thighs to allow for easy movement. Thumbing through them, my hand stopped at a pair of cargo pants. They were one size bigger than my normal, but they were black and had plenty of pockets. *Some extra room might be a good thing*, I thought.

"I'm so sorry, Miss Vickie," a young girl, maybe twenty or twenty-one, seemed to beg for forgiveness as she rushed through the front door. She hurriedly put on her blue worker's vest as she went to the time clock near an office door toward the left side of the building. "I'm so sorry."

A middle-aged woman stepped out of the small office with her hands on her hips. "Look here, you are a good worker and I like you. But you need to figure some better transportation or I'm gonna have to let you go."

The loud metallic click sounded as her time card was punched. "My boy was sick this morning and my momma couldn't make it to my apartment in time for me to catch the bus. I'm sorry. It won't happen again." She stood submissively in front of the Vickie woman with her eyes down to the floor.

She was panting, I could see.

I watched the scene unfold from over the racks of clothes with the pair of cargo pants draped over my arm.

Vickie asked, "So, how did you get here? It took you twenty-five minutes."

The young girl simply answered, "I ran. I ran here, Miss Vickie."

I didn't know that girl at all and I'd never been in her predicament. Her determination, though, it was amazing.

Vickie fussed, "Get to work. We have some new inventory," before disappearing into the small office room.

I ended up with the one pair of black cargo pants, a black t-shirt, a sports bra, and a pair of dark grey running shoes, and also an old backpack that I managed to find shoved deep inside a bin of luggage, black of course.

The young girl saw me approaching the counter and shuffled to the front. "I'm coming, Miss," she said.

Laying everything out for her to scan, I couldn't help but start up the conversation, "Hey, I overheard you talking earlier. You seriously ran here?"

"Yes, I had to. It's just me and Bobby, that's my little boy. He's two. He has some issues. And dang-it, I missed the transit bus again. I'm not always late, only maybe once a week. But once a week is just too often. I know that. I'll try harder." She nodded to herself as she folded the two t-shirts. "You want these in a sack or in the backpack?"

"The backpack is fine."

"Anyway, things'll get better. I know they will."

I smiled and handed her the fourteen dollars.

Popping the trunk of the Toyota Camry, I set the backpack inside, and I just stood there. Thinking.

A plastic Walmart sack was already in the trunk containing some socks and underclothes along with two boxes of ammo.

Thinking of Mom again … and this car, I turned around, leaned my backside up against the trunk and took in some of the scenery. It was nice here. Not fancy and new San Diego, more of an older area. Although, it had its charm. The scent of the salt water was in the air, but no waterfront was visible from where I stood.

With my mind made up, I whirled around, shoved the two boxes of ammo into the bottom of the new backpack, followed by the sack of underclothes. Shutting the trunk, I climbed into the back seat, worked my hand inside the secret access slit, and pulled out the long Sig Sauer nine-millimeter with its silencer. Holding it low and out of sight, I carefully unscrewed the silencer and placed each piece in the backpack among the clothes.

Once satisfied it was safely packed away, I climbed over the center console and into the passenger seat. The moment caught me off guard. I'd not been in this seat since that day at the gas station. In this seat, staring out of the cracked glass, I felt like that child again. Closing my eyes, I could still see her through the windshield standing at the counter of the store when the man ran into it with a shotgun. It was so many years ago, but I never did get over her death and I never will completely. I closed my eyes in a useless effort to hold the tears in. This car was my last connection with her. *I can't do it. I can't.*

Slowly, I unlatched the glove box and let it drop open. Inside was only a single folded piece of paper, the car's title. My trembling hands retrieved and unfolded it. I flipped it over to see her signature. Her handwriting. Tilting my head back, looking up at the tan headliner, I told myself that this was best. Mom would agree.

Yes, it was the right choice. I felt for the thirty-eight still stuffed between my back and jeans in the small of my back and stepped out with the backpack, the key, and the folded car title.

When I walked back inside the store, the young girl immediately came to me. "Is everything ok? Was there a mistake?"

"No, no mistake," I said.

Her face took on a confused expression. "Then ..."

I interrupted her, "Do you see that car out there? The blue Camry?"

"Yes," she answered. "Do you need a jump? Is it broken? I can call somebody if you need."

"No, it runs just fine." I reached toward her with the key and paper. "It's yours. You can have it."

She backed away a step and held up her hands. "No, no. I can't."

Reaching forward, I grabbed her right hand and placed the key and paper in it. "Yes, you can have it. That paper is the title. There's the key. It's paid for. It runs. It's yours."

She was sobbing and holding the key and title with both hands against her chest when I walked out.

chapter eighteen

The new me walked into the San Diego airport somewhat nervous. With my backpack over one shoulder, I entered through the automatic doors following three strangers. Just inside, I stopped at a large mirror hung on the wall.

Turning squarely at the mirror and my own reflection, I did believe that I had succeeded. The young lady looking back at me with shoulder-length, pitch-black hair, dark mascara, and dressed in all black, looked nothing like the well-clothed, long brown haired assistant attorney Kaitlyn Cline from a middle class life. Staring back at me was Kait Falcon, a grown-up version of the hurt little girl who used the dark gothic appearance to hide the pain of loss from her childhood.

I slipped the small wallet with my new ID out of my front pants pocket observing the picture and the name on it. Needing to get used to the alias Elmore's assistant made up for me, I mouthed my new name to myself to hear the ring of it, *Sarah Rilley*. The person staring back at me in the mirror did not look like a Sarah, though. But it would do.

Behind the ID was the one credit card Elmore had assigned me and two crumpled receipts, one from a bakery and one from the FedEx center. I smiled to the girl in the mirror, feeling good about my deception and the hope that it'd work. After meeting with Elmore again early yesterday morning, I found a bakery and purchased two carrot cakes, a large one and a medium one. I wrapped the nine-mil, the little thirty-eight, and ammo in plastic bags. The nine along with its silencer was hidden inside the larger cake and my tiny thirty-eight inside the medium, along with the two boxes of ammo.

I packed them up and the guy at the FedEx office promised that my cakes would be safely delivered to my North Carolina hotel by the time of my arrival.

As I walked away from the mirror and toward the ticket kiosk, I pulled the phone from my back pocket and dialed Dad. He picked up after a few rings and asked how things went with Elmore. I told him all went well, I had an ID, and some funds to last me until I got my issue settled, hopefully soon, I added. I told him what I did with the car and that I was now at the airport getting ready to take off for North Carolina.

"What about the Sig and little Pico?" he asked.

I pressed the appropriate buttons on the ticket kiosk and waited for my printed boarding pass. "I shipped them to a hotel inside some food items."

"Good, good," he affirmed.

Walking along the path toward security, I broke the boring conversation and asked, "Dad, did Mom work with you?"

"What do mean?"

I settled in behind a small line of people waiting to have their bags and bodies scanned. "Oh, come on, Dad. The truth. Elmore said that she was a good team member?" I shuffled along with the line. Two more people now behind me. "Did she do what you did?"

His answer was flat, "Yeah, Kait, she did."

"I'm gonna have to go in a second. But was her death at that store a random event? Or, was it … you know?" I glanced around me. No one seemed to be listening to me, but I had to pick my words carefully. "Dad, tell me."

"No, Kait. I don't feel it was a random robbery."

"Then who?" I asked.

"I have no idea. Coulda' been just about anyone. I had my suspicions back then, but … We'll talk about that later. Ok?"

"Ok. Bye, Dad," I said. "I'll call you in a day or two."

I emptied my pockets and laid the backpack in the plastic bin, then stepped through the metal detector. The bin rolled along the rails past me and another security agent waved me on through, motioning for me to take my bag.

Finding a seat near departure gate 32, I sat and waited.

chapter nineteen

The announcement over the loudspeaker was a welcome sound. "We will be landing at Charlotte Douglas International Airport in one hour. The time in Charlotte, North Carolina, will be 9:06pm."

Charlotte Douglas, CLT as the airlines call it, is one of the busiest airports in the US, just under the top ten, and only forty-five minutes from my house. I flew out of that same airport ten very long days ago. My social status of a car should still be there in the long-term parking. Ten days ago, driving a Mercedes made me feel important, successful, and as if I'd achieved a status, even though I'd bought it second-hand. I had worked so hard to be a success and did my damned best to make it look that way. Funny how quickly our lives can change. How easily a life can be taken away.

I was a workaholic, as some would say. Long hours at the office helped me to climb the ladder, get better clients, and become known.

Daniel was honestly the glue that held our family together. He made sure the girls got to school everyday on time. Packed their lunches and washed the clothes. Often cooking dinner day after day for days on end after getting home from his job as an accountant because I wasn't there.

There'd be days when I'd leave early and get back late, not seeing the girls at all. It's hard to look at yourself and pick out your own negative flaws, but after being gone so long and knowing that they have no idea if I'm alive or not, picking out my flaws gets pretty easy. I wonder, have they given up on me yet? How long will it be before they do? How soon will they go on with their normal lives and routines? I felt my eyes begin to water. Truthfully, their lives wouldn't be much different. I was never there anyway. *Fuck, I need to talk to them*, my mind screamed. *I need to let them know I'm ok.*

I need to let them know I'm ok ... before they ... forget me. Leaning forward in my seat, I laid my head in the palms of hands and I cried. I really cried.

I'd get this finished quickly, walk in the door and hug Daniel, Mattie, Olivia. I'd forget these last few days ever happened. Then I'd change. Be home more. Work a little less. Sell that expensive socialite car, if it's even still in the airport parking lot anyway.

Maybe Dad's right. And maybe I'm wrong in thinking that bringing information to the police will make this nightmare go away. Maybe Dad is right. Maybe I do need to eliminate the threat.

With only the black backpack over my shoulder, I walked out of the airport and flagged the first cab I saw. "To the La Quinta near Interstates Seventy-Seven and Two-Eighty-Seven," I told the driver.

He leaned toward the open window trying to spy if I had any other luggage. "You have no bags?"

"Nope," I replied, already climbing in the back seat.

"Okie dokie," he said.

I settled in and lazily leaned my body into the door panel, watching the city lights go by. I knew I didn't have long, maybe a twenty-five minute ride.

The hotel sign showed itself before the cab driver gave me his broken English notification. My office was only five blocks from this La Quinta, and why I picked it. My normal everyday drive would bring me right past this hotel heading into the office each morning and then back home, usually well after dark.

He pulled up under the brightly-lit entrance and pointed to his meter, "This is you charge ma'am."

I handed him my credit card and said, "Go ahead and add a couple dollars for letting me use the card."

"Thank you," he said. "Very nice of you. You have good day."

"You too," I said, opening the door.

The cab sped away to his next fare and I remained where I stood, taking in the parking lot. Looking for anything out of place. I was still a bit nervous about the package I'd sent here.

Inside, a lady wearing a red shirt and nice blue blazer jacket welcomed me from behind the counter. "Good evening, do you have a reservation with us?"

"I do," answering as I made my way toward her. "Sarah Rilley."

She tapped away at her keyboard. "Ah yes, here you are."

My heart skipped a beat. What if somehow the true contents of my package were known? I waited for some pause in her voice or worry in her eye. Nothing.

"Oh, I have a note here for me to give you a package upon your arrival." She turned on her heels rather quickly and went into a small room behind the counter. I stepped back and checked my exit just in case. She returned carrying a box, the same box I had packed. "It says there's a food product in here. I hope it made the trip ok?"

Walking forward again, I dropped my ID on the counter and took the box, cradling it under my arm.

She handed me the receipt and key, smiled, and told me to have a wonderful stay and that checkout was at eleven and breakfast would start at nine-thirty.

The hotel room was as plain as they come. Basic, cheap, and with no extra guest amenities. Two queen beds, a desk screwed to the wall and one roller chair. The room was dark despite the two lamps. It had tan walls, dark burgundy curtains with that wholesale dark-red wooden furniture. Definitely not high style. I flipped the deadbolt and the swing-lock, twisted and tugged the door handle once to be sure, then sat on one of the beds with my box of cakes. In the closed space of the room with no air movement, I could smell the cakes as soon as I tore open the first flap of the box.

"Hmm," I said aloud to myself, "maybe I shoulda' picked better cakes. I don't even like carrot cake that much."

Digging the weapons and ammo boxes out of the bottom of the cakes was somewhat messier than the job of getting them in there. I did take a couple bites of cake. It wasn't good, but I was hungry. Removing the two pistols and silencer from their plastic bags, I carefully laid them on the bed and helped myself to some more cake.

10:11pm. The small clock glowed red on the table between the beds.

I sat there on the bed and stared at myself in the big mirror. Thinking about what was next. My office. The office wasn't anything to brag about. We were only a small branch. We had no security cameras or alarm system. Getting in would be easy. The keypad on the door had only one code that myself and three others used.

The cleaning crew would be done by midnight.

Finding any clue of why someone wanted me dead was going to be the hard part.

I'd wait until 2am. That'd be a good time to go in.

Setting the alarm on my phone, I fell back on the bed and closed my eyes. Shortly before dozing off, I let my fingers find the little thirty-eight and slip it under my thigh.

chapter twenty

Carrying only the tiny thirty-eight placed again between my skin and pants at the small of my back, I made the short walk to my office. It was on Belmont Avenue, a street that sounds much fancier than it actually is. Two in the morning was an interesting time to be walking around a city. I'd say the most quiet time. It was too late for anyone who's up to no good to be out and too early for those first-shift workers making their commute.

I kept to the sidewalks for my trip. No use attracting attention from any security cameras by taking shortcuts.

The office was a stand-alone, small single-story building built in the eighties from cinder blocks that had been painted over so many times that the texture of the cement was no longer visible. It was a light grey color that nearly matched the concrete of the parking lot. Just before we leased it, someone tried to liven up the place with some landscaping and small juniper trees planted in the grass area between the parking and the door. The work did help the appearance somewhat. Although, at this hour under the street lights, the juniper trees cast dark shadows onto the narrow walkway to the door, creating a blackened space in which I couldn't see anything as I approached. I walked steadily toward the door with my right hand behind my back, lightly clasping the thirty-eight's handgrip.

A beam of light crossed the parking lot from right to left as a lone car made a turn onto the street. Judging from the path of light, the car was heading up the street to my left. I quickened my pace and made my way into a shadow just as it passed.

With the light from my cellphone, I punched in the code, opened the door, and slipped in softly, pulling the door closed behind me. My office was second down on the left. No need to flip on any lights, there was enough of a glow from the street lights filtering in through the closed blinds to navigate the building.

My office had the same glow coming in from its one window. All my stuff was just as I had left it. At least my coworkers hadn't given up on me yet. A pile of mail lay near the far edge. Powering up the desktop computer, I sat down in my familiar office chair and rolled it up to the desk. It almost felt like normal sitting there waiting on the computer to load up, except for the bulge from the thirty-eight at my back, hitting the lumbar support of the chair.

I began my search with the files of recently-closed cases. Rarely do I remember case numbers, but defendant's names, I do. I skipped those cases where the defendant was acquitted or deemed not-guilty and carefully studied those who were found guilty.

What was each defendant's personality like? How did he or she behave during trial? Do I remember them making me feel uncomfortable? It was a challenge to sit there and look at each name and attempt to play back their entire trial and every communication with them looking for clues. Did I miss what could be perceived as a threat? Was he or she overly angry? Of course, everyone who ends up guilty is angry, but there are some who feel they've been wronged by the judge, jury, or attorney.

Going back through six months of cases in and hour and a half, I'd hit a wall. None of them stood out. In many of those guilty verdicts, the defendant actually admitted, in some way, that they'd done the crime. That was always a great place from which to start a case. I'd push for the top end of the mandatory sentence while their defense attempted to prove the lesser end was all that was needed.

With a thump, I laid my head down on the wooden desktop. My fingers tapping the blank plastic space on the keyboard in a rhythm to help me think.

If not any of these, then who?

I have no life other than work and home. If not any of these ...

It just can't be.

It can't be Daniel. It can't. That doesn't make any sense in my mind. And why? We haven't fought. I'm not having an affair. I doubt he is. I hope he isn't. I'm never home, though. This job is my life.

I probably shouldn't be surprised if he *is* having an affair. I missed our last anniversary because I was interviewing some guy's boss late one night after his shift ended.

I can remember when Daniel would complain about my crazy work hours in his sweet, non-accusing way. In the mornings, he'd ask if I'd be home for supper and before I could even reply, he could sense my answer and he'd simply look down at the floor and say ok.
Lately, he doesn't even ask anymore.

People always say that those closest to things can never see the truth. Subtle clues get missed, like the hints hidden within comments and conversations. Am *I* missing something? Have *I* done so much damage in my family life that only by my complete nonexistence would Daniel and the girls be better off?

I couldn't let my mind keep running along with those thoughts. It just didn't add up. I picked my head up, rolled my eyes to the ceiling, and bit the very edge of my lip. I was blank. I had nothing. The computer screen had gone black. I flicked the mouse with my index finger and the screen came alive again in the dark room.

Those most recent cases left me with no better insight and I had no new cases coming up. The Aspen trip was a break for me, sort of. I went there to deliver files to a victim's family. I always felt better doing that in person. It was a chance to get away, and I took it.

With the room lit by only the computer monitor, I reached for the pile of mail and slid it in front of me. A useless endeavor, I knew, but it was a habit. On top of the stack was the most recent office memo. Next were two bills, and below that was a copy of the American Bar Association journal. Then, a copy of the Charlotte Observer and below that, an issue of Paralegal Today. Piling everything back just as it was, something caught my eye. A post-it note. Flipping back to the Charlotte Observer newspaper, there was a small yellow post-it note stuck over the main headline.

The writing on the note only read, *Check this out*. The date of the paper was from Thursday, June 5th, the day I flew out to Colorado. I lifted the note and read the headline.

```
Philip Bianchi, nephew of suspected drug-lord,
    arrested on charges of money laundering.
```

Reading further...

```
Local authorities along with the FBI have
arrested the nephew of Matteo Bianchi on
```

charges of money laundering. The arrest of Philip Bianchi may provide evidence to bring down what is believed to be one of the largest drug importers on the central eastern coast.

    Mr. Bianchi's arraignment will be held at United States District Court in Charlotte next Tuesday.

I slowly replaced the post-it note back over the headline, re-stacked the pile of mail, and pushed it back to its original location.

chapter twenty-one

A new lady was at the hotel counter upon my return. Her disposition was so happy, it was almost infectious. "Well, good morning," she cheerfully said as I entered and took a sharp left into the hall. "Hope you had a wonderful evening out."

"I did. Thank you," I answered with a grin.

Shutting and locking my room door behind me, I immediately went into the bathroom and reached up underneath the sink to retrieve the Sig Sauer nine-mil from where I stashed it. I'd jammed it on top of some of the plumbing pipes.

My phone alarm woke me at 10am, giving me a one hour time window for a shower and breakfast before a phone call to San Diego which was a three hour time gap. The call would greet Elmore as he walked into his office in Cali.

The warm water running down my skin was hypnotizing. With the strong spray massaging me, I let myself relax in the moment, forgetting the world awaiting me outside of this faux marble enclosure. My feeling of safety only enhanced by the clear plastic bag beside me on the shower shelf. Through the frosty, water-droplet covered plastic, the thirty-eight laid there at the ready.

Lightly rubbing my hands up and down my wet, naked body, I could feel a difference. The muscle tone was evident. The exercise, lower caloric intake, and more moving around were beginning to transform me back into my younger self. Letting my hands move through the beading water up from my thighs, past my buttocks, and into the shallow crease in the center of my lower back, I felt the bump there. It had scarred over and was now only a small imperfection where the bullet entered on that morning on the mountain. Moving my right hand over, the exit wound was somewhat larger and still gave off a slight tingle when I pressed my finger to it.

The wounds themselves kept my anger from fading away. Emotions and feelings tend to subside over time. It's only natural. We eventually become less emotional to life events or losses as the days pass by and we settle into an acceptance of what has happened and we move on. These two wounds, though. They'll serve as constant reminders. Not reminders of what happened that morning, but reminders of what I have to lose.

I rinsed my pitch-black hair one more time, turned the shower knob off, and stood there. Shivering a little, small goose-bumps began to form over my skin.

I'm still alive and I plan to stay that way.

I was barely out of the shower when my fingers hit the saved number I'd put in for Elmore Williams' office. Monica, his front desk assistant, answered quickly, "Hi, Kait, how are you this morning?"

"I'm good. Is Elmore around?"

Without hesitation, she said, "Yes, he is. I'll transfer you now."

Only a couple seconds went by then he picked up. "Good morning, Kait. Are you finding any answers?"

"I think so," I replied. "Could I have you look something up for me?"

"Sure."

"I need to know some information. In North Carolina, a man named Philip Bianchi was arrested recently." I paused a moment, remembering that I had not told him about my job, my home, or my married name. "I need to know what law firm is prosecuting him. Is that something you can find out?"

In a fatherly tone, Elmore answered, "I think we can accomplish that for you. I'll have Monica find out as soon as she can and call you with the result. I'm guessing this piece of intelligence will help you to arrive one step closer to a final conclusion?"

"I do believe so."

"Very well then. Monica'll be in touch," Elmore said before disconnecting.

Hanging up, I slipped on my cargo pants and sports bra, then went to the desk chair near the window, bringing the nine-millimeter with me. The gun still amazed me. Slouching back in the chair as a teenager does and using my foot to twist it back and forth, I studied the pistol. The checkered hand gripping and metalwork were so perfect. Every part fit together with precision. Modern machinery at its finest. My thumb pressed the button to release the magazine out from the bottom of the handgrip and with my left hand, I slowly took hold of the top slide-action, pulling it back to release the one shell in the chamber. It sprung out and landed on the stained blue carpet under me.

I twisted the chair toward the window and kicked the bottom corner of the heavy curtain aside with my foot. Light flooded into the room as the curtain settled back down, leaving about eight inches of the outside world visible. Taking aim with the unloaded nine-mil, I let its sights follow the few pedestrians walking on the sidewalk across the street. The exercise was to mentally prepare for my true target, whose name I did not know yet.

With the sights, I traced each pedestrians' every stride, anticipating when they'd stop, slow down, or look at their phone. Figuring out which trigger pull would lead to the most precise and deadly shot.

A person walks at a constant pace for their body. One may walk faster than the next, but when watching one person intently, the pattern shows up. They may slow for a moment, such as when avoiding another pedestrian or stepping down from a curb, but their body will subconsciously attempt to resume its pre-programmed pace. It's hardly noticeable, but there's a quickened movement just after a person slows down for something. That timeframe could lead to a vital miss at three or four hundred feet. A miss that would be hugely important not only since my target would have not been eliminated, my target would then know that they were, in fact, a target.

Watching more people walk about their daily lives through my room's dirty windowpane, I practiced keeping track of them along with their surroundings. I needed to focus on more than just the pedestrian. A piece of paper blowing across the ground, a passing car, a kid on a bicycle. Any of those things would create an unanticipated action or reaction in my target that would lead to a misplaced bullet.

My mental practice was shattered by the ring of my cell phone. It was Elmore's number. "Hello," I answered, letting the nine-mil come to rest in my lap.

Monica began in her professional tone. "Kait, I have the answer you were requesting."

"Yes," I said.

"The law firm that is prosecuting the case of Philip Bianchi is called McGillis and Associates. It is located in Charlotte, North Carolina on Belmont Avenue in the central area of town. Do you know this law firm?"

A cold chill went through me with the realization. It was my office prosecuting him. My chest began to rise and fall noticeably as my heart rate picked up. I had to give Monica an answer, though. Calmly, I replied, "No, Monica, never heard of them. But I'll check them out."

She added, "They are handling the case for the DA's office. If there is anything else you need, feel free to give us a call."

"Ok, thanks," I said, letting the phone fall loosely from my hand onto my thigh.

"Shit." I said aloud. "So much for the misdemeanors and petty crimes. But still, no one with any brains in their head would put an obvious hit on their prosecuting attorney right after a case has been assigned." Rotating the chair side to side as if that would shake my brain up, I continued talking out loud to myself. "Shit. This isn't making any sense."

I stewed over that for nearly an hour, coming to no real conclusions. Eventually, I gave up the chair and began to pace the room. My thought had been that moving around and getting my blood pumping would somehow help, but no. Fifteen laps in, while passing the desk, I picked up my cell phone. Without breaking my stride across the carpet, I woke the phone and went to my contacts which only had two numbers in it, Dad's and Elmore's. I touched Dad's name and waited.

"Kait, how are you?" he asked.

"Hey, Dad, I'm good. Well, as good as I can be given the last few days." My body kept my stride as I talked and circled the room blindly.

He went straight to the point. "Are you figuring anything out?"

"Sort of," I answered. Then I went on to tell him about Philip Bianchi's arrest and that my firm was handed his case to prosecute. And that I'd read books and seen TV shows where a defendant killed someone on the prosecution team. But that was fiction. It was simply too obvious in real life. I asked him how dumb would someone be to try that.

He listened intently and gave a couple *uh-huh*'s through the deal.

"Well, what do you think of that?" I asked.

Dad wasn't joking, but asked me back that same question in a sarcastic way. "Kait, what *you* think of that?"

"Dad, I don't know. Like I said, it doesn't make any sense."

"Let me ask you …," he said. "Who would gain the most if Philip Bianchi and his uncle were out of the picture?"

"What do you mean?" I blurted.

"I meant just what I said. Who would benefit the most if those two were gone and in jail for money laundering, drug trafficking, and murder of a state attorney?"

"I guess every other drug dealer."

"Yes," he said quietly.

My mind started to follow along better. "So, I need to know who is Matteo Bianchi's closest rival or competition."

"Now you're coming around," he said.

I began to ramble to Dad in the phone. "The newspaper said that Matteo is believed to be one of the largest importers on the East Coast. I don't need to worry about small-time guys, there has to be another large importer who would get that business if Matteo went under. Right? I've just got to find out who that would be. Yeah, that's the next step. Thanks a bunch, Dad."

"Anytime, my girl. We'll talk later."

Tossing my phone onto the bed, I plopped back into the desk chair.

I'm no CIA or government investigator, but I've read stories about how those guys take months and years to catch a drug boss. They start small by buying drugs from the guys on the street, build trust and begin to ask about purchasing larger quantities. Over the long haul of forming relationships, they finally figure out who the head-honcho is and go in for a bust after piling up stacks of evidence. My problem is that I just don't have that kind of time. I need to know now.

chapter twenty-two

In downtown Charlotte exists a non-franchise electronics store. I'd never been there. Only heard about it. Besides the normal tech such as phones, gaming systems and such, they carried less innocent devices such as tiny security cameras meant to be hidden and trackers. GPS trackers. The detectives in town often visited the store for supplies, or so I'd been told.

  I turned in my hotel room key, asked the counter lady to call me a taxi, and took a chocolate Hersey candy from the basket as I left the lobby to wait outside. My thirty-eight was tucked in its usual place and the nine-mil was disassembled and wrapped up in socks inside my backpack.

  The taxi was quick. He pulled up with his passenger window down. "Where to?" he asked.

  "K&R Electronics and Hobby on fifth, then the Greyhound bus station."

  He motioned with his head to get in.

K&R Electronics and Hobby was a much bigger store than I'd imagined. The taxi pulled into a parking space near the entrance. Just inside the front windows were four large radio controlled airplanes. They were hanging on thin strings from the ceiling at various angles replicating how'd they'd look in flight.

"Wait here," I told the cabbie. "I may be a little while and ... yeah, I know, I'll pay for your wait." I held two dollar bills across his seat and said, "Here, go over there to that gas station and get a drink or something."

I made sure to bring along my backpack. The doorbell rang as I entered. Oddly, not an electronic bell, it was literally a brass bell on a string tied to the interior door handle. Aisles and aisles of shelving were crammed into the space. I stopped for a moment to look around. Soldering irons and bins of tiny sliver and brass circuit board stuff were to the left and the shelving to the right held other trinkets such as little motors, plastic parts, wheels and tires for motorized toy cars, and so much more of which I had no idea.

"I'm back here if you need help," a voice sounded from the middle left of the store.

Walking toward the voice, I passed the phones and radios before coming to an opening in the shelving where there was a desk up against the wall. A kid about twenty or so was at the desk working on something. Something small. He heard me approach him from behind. "Just one second." He laid a tiny screwdriver down and spun around saying, "Hi, can I help you?"

"Do you guys have a small GPS tracking device?"

"We do. I'll need to know what you're wanting to track to help you better. Do you need it for a kid's backpack, a dog, a car, a person?"

"A person?" The question blurted out of me. "Can you track a person?"

He stood and stuffed the tips of fingers into his pant's pockets. "Yes, for customers who have older relatives with dementia or Alzheimers. You know, those older people who have problems with walking off and not knowing where they are?"

"Ah, yes." My head bounced slightly as my brain understood. "Oh, a car. I need it for a truck actually. I'm letting a cousin borrow my pickup for a trip. I just want to have a device on it in case something happens." I stood by for his response.

He nodded saying, "Ok, I can set you up with that. Let's go over here." He took off to the back of the store. "You know," he said, looking back over his shoulder, "I read that Dodge trucks are one of the most stolen vehicles.

"Is that right? I wouldn't have guessed."

With his back to me, he asked, "Is yours a Dodge?"

"My what?"

"Your truck. The one your cousin is borrowing."

"No. It's a Chevy," I replied, not really all that familiar with either brand of pickups.

He came to a sudden stop in front of a shelf. "Here we are. I've got quite an assortment to choose from." His finger went from one to the other, hanging on the metal pegs. "Got short range, long range, cheap, expensive. But if you need it for your Chevy, you'll need a long range one, right?"

"Right."

He pointed to one in particular and told me, "It isn't very cheap, but that one there is probably the best. Good magnets to stick against the metal and all you need is a SIM card. No monthly subscription or anything like that."

"Ok, I'll give it a go then," I said, pulling it from its hanger. "Will you show me how to use it?"

"Yes, I can," he answered with a suspicious grin.

The taxi driver had his head back and eyes closed listening to the radio when I came out. His elbow hung relaxed out of the driver's side window. When I shut the back door, he opened his eyes, looking at me in the rearview mirror. "You got everything you needed, ma'am?"

"I did. I hope you didn't mind the wait."

"Nope, not at all. Got me a nice little nap on your bill." He straightened up and cranked the engine. "You said the Greyhound station. Is that right?"

"Yes, but I've got a detour," I said. "I want to drive by an address first."

"Are you getting down there too?"

I shook my head in reply as he eyed me in the mirror. "No, just a drive-by. The address is 410 Bowmer Lane."

He pulled out of the parking lot. "Ok, got it. You enjoy the ride."

I sat back and fixed my gaze out of the window and said in a low voice, "I will. I will."

My body tensed up as the taxi rounded the last left hand turn. I lowered myself in the seat, making it to the point I could barely see out of the window. "Slow down some, please," I said.

He slowed, but it still felt so fast. Daniel's car was in the driveway and no one was visible in the front of the house as we approached. However, as the taxi passed the house, I could see into our small back yard. My eyes watered up the moment I saw them. Both of them. Mattie and Olivia kicking a soccer ball back and forth on the grass. Then their images disappeared as the taxi rolled on down the street.

Two seconds.

That was only two seconds that I desperately needed to last forever. I closed my eyes in an effort to keep the vision alive.

With my eyes still closed, I could virtually feel the awkwardness in the taxi and I somehow knew that the driver was studying me again in the rearview mirror. I could feel it.

Opening my eyes, I noticed him glancing up to the mirror and back at the road in repetition. Finally, he asked, "Did you know those girls?"

"No, I didn't. Only the house."

He seemed relieved to end the silence and asked, "You used to live there?"

"Yeah, I used to," I said, turning my head to watch the rest of the neighborhood go by. "It feels like so long ago."

chapter twenty-three

I'd never ridden on a Greyhound bus. Never needed to. Until now. I needed to get away from this town, from the temptation of contacting Daniel and the girls, but I had no need to go too far … not yet. Not until I found out exactly where my mystery person called home.

What I do know, though, is that the bus is slow but cheap. And best of all, they don't check bags.

I stepped out of the cab after the driver handed me back my credit card and gave me farewell. "Thank you, Miss Sarah. Good day."

I waved and walked into the station. A spacious open floor of boring grey concrete took up one side of the large building while rows of vinyl-covered chairs occupied the other side. Making a mental note of the five people scattered in the chairs, I went to the ticket window. "Raleigh," I said, handing the woman my card and ID.

In short order, the woman handed everything back, "Ok, here is your pass and cards. The bus will be leaving in twenty minutes. Last one of the day. Have an enjoyable trip."

Taking a seat in the far right corner, second to last row with no one behind me or out of my vision, I stretched out and watched two other people meander through the entrance door up to the ticket window.

Daydreaming about my next move to solve this personal puzzle of mine, I began to watch a little girl eleven rows in front of me and third seat from the right. She looked to be about my girls' age. Cute and proper, not spoiled but not a street kid either. A small luggage bag was in the seat next to her. Her attention was fixed upon the pages of the book she was reading. She wore a plaid skirt, light blue blouse and her legs were appropriately crossed at the ankles just as the young lady she must have been raised to be.

I let out a shallow laugh thinking about how much of an opposite I was to her. Sitting here, sprawled out very non-lady-like, in black cargos with my black shoulder-length hair that was cut in a hotel bathroom and a torso-hugging black t-shirt to match. The only contrast to my appearance being my light skin due to too many hours sitting at an office desk.

As the two new-comers found themselves a seat, I noticed the man five rows in front of me. Clean-shaven, respectable in appearance. His back was to me. He faced the little girl. He watched her. Intently.

I scooted my ass into my chair and sat more upright. I crossed one leg over the other knee and leaned into the metal armrest, paying more attention to the scene playing out in front of me.

The little girl was oblivious to his stare. He was oblivious to mine. Every so often, she'd look up to the clock on the side wall and each time, the man would look away. His gaze returned only when she went back into the pages of her book.

I wondered, was I being watched like that in Aspen? Was I just as oblivious to something right in front of me like this girl was? Was I really that easy of a target? Too caught up in my own world to notice the obvious?

The man gathered up a small bag and a magazine and stood. The little girl made no note. He walked over to her, taking a chair just on the other side of her luggage bag.

I sat up straight as a board and pulled my own backpack into my lap, carefully unzipping the main compartment.

The man said something to her and she smiled. No words were audible from my distance, but I could tell that she mouthed, *thank you* to him. Her attention returned to her book. The man kept his eye to her, studying her as she read. Her body shifted away from him, dropping her inside shoulder a tiny bit. Never taking her eyes off of her book. He said something else and she made quick eye contact, responding with a few words or a sentence. I couldn't tell for sure.

With both hands inside the backpack in my lap, I slipped the nine millimeter out of its sock and did the same with its silencer.

The man leaned in toward her, placing his arm over the backs of both chairs. Only the chair with her luggage was between them. His hand falling onto the back of the girl's. She pushed herself farther into the distant corner of her chair. She pressed up against the armrest. Her eyes still on the book. Her attention on the man carefully and purposefully invading her personal space.

He leaned in a little more.

I screwed the silencer onto the nine-mil and inserted the loaded clip into the bottom of the handgrip.

Her body language displaying full discomfort.

The man smiled.

She did not. Her shoulders squirmed and drew in submissively. Closing her book, she said something to the man without facing him.

He nodded.

I arranged the nine-mil on top of everything in my backpack with the grip toward the outer edge.

Leaving her luggage bag and her book, the little girl excused herself to the man and walked toward a wide hallway at the far end. I could see the restroom signs in the shadow of the hall and an exit door further beyond.

She entered that hallway and turned left, out of sight. The man's neck craned watching her, and as soon as she turned left, he hastily rose and followed in her direction.

I stood and slipped my backpack on. Reaching behind me with my right hand, I made sure that I'd left the zipper opened just enough to get my hand inside.

As I approached the left turn in what seemed to be a wide and long hallway, I took a broad berth to ensure that I could see any surprise that may be waiting just beyond the corner. Midway down the hall, light from an open room on the right spilled into the hallway and onto the man creating an eerie silhouette. At the very end was the sign hanging to designate the women's room.

He shot me a quick, expressionless look. I imagine that he wasn't expecting another visitor to his little party.

Walking past him, I held my breath, kept my eyes to the floor, and my ears tuned for any sound that would indicate a movement from him.

Once inside the restroom, I scanned the stall doors, seeing her shoes in the last one. The latch clicked open and the door opened. I stopped in my tracks, gave a good-natured grin and asked, "Hey, can I ask you a question?"

She crossed the tile floor to a sink and rinsed her hands. "Yeah, sure," she answered, drying off on her skirt.

"Do you know that guy out there? The one who was sitting next to you?"

Her eyes widened. "No, I don't. He's kinda creepy. Asked me if I was traveling alone, and how old I was. Do you know him?"

I paused, not knowing what to say next. Her eyes focused on mine, waiting for an answer from me, I told her, "I think I've seen him around before. He's outside in the hall." Lost for words, or at least anything to say that would make sense, I went for a shot in the dark. "He might be some salesman. Tell you what, I'll walk out with you and ask him a couple questions. You go on out to your seat in the main lobby, ok."

"Ok," she replied hesitantly.

The man's hopes visibly faded away when he saw me walk out of the restroom with the little girl side by side. She walked briskly and nervously as I guided her with my arm around her shoulder. When we were directly in front of him, I said pleasantly to her, "You go on to your seat now."

I then came to a halt and faced him. He quickly turned his head back and forth between her walking around the corner and me standing right in front of him.

"Who are you?" I asked. "Why are you bugging her?"

"Leave me the fuck alone," he hissed. "She's my …"

I interrupted, "She doesn't know you."

His eyes turned pure evil.

"Give me your ID," I demanded, holding out my hand but knowing he'd never hand it over.

His right hand went to his back pocket and then, I only saw a flash of light. A reflection.

Instinct took over and my left arm went up to block his strike, my head ducking to the right just in case. When his forearm collided with mine, I went in with a right fist into his sternum.

He stumbled back.

I heard a metallic sound hit the floor.

Catching hold of his sleeve with my left, I sent my right fist in again — to his throat. It was a high hit for me, but he wasn't a real fighter. The neck hit was a painful surprise and both of his hands quickly went to his neck to prevent another throat strike.

I reached up with both hands, grabbed handfuls of hair in each and yanked down while twisting my body into him. The motion sent him face first onto the floor in the doorway of the open room. Some blood splatter glistened in the light next to the knife that had fallen from his grasp moments earlier.

Taking a glance down the hall and not seeing anyone, I stepped in front of him as he was getting his arms underneath his body to push himself up. I took hold of another two handfuls of hair and dragged him into the open room. He grunted and squirmed using one elbow to keep himself off of the concrete and the other to slap at my fists which were tightly intertwined into his hair.

Once out of sight of the hallway, I slammed his face down onto the concrete one more bloody time before letting go. He rolled over. Any fight left in him was gone. Blood trickled down his face from a gash in his forehead and both nostrils.

I reached behind me into the backpack and came out with the nine-mil. His eyes flinched at the sight of it and followed its movement. Kneeling down at his side, I slowly traced his body with the end of the silencer coming to a stop at his crotch. I pressed down hard with the round metal tube while watching his fear. His lip trembled and his eyes pleaded his silent request.

"Give me your ID," I said, repeating my command from the beginning.

He began to work his left arm behind him to his pant's pocket. I pressed the nine-mil's silencer down harder into his groin. A twitching hand resurfaced holding a tattered brown leather wallet.

Lifting the nine-millimeter and snatching the wallet, I stood up, towering over him. "Get out," I ordered.

His eyes remained fixed on his wallet in my hand without a word as if he were wanting to ask for it back.

"Get out."

I stepped aside to give him room and he hurriedly got up, scampering out into the hall and to the left out the back door. Placing the nine-mil back into its hiding place, I saw the knife still on the hall floor. I dared not touch it for fear of fingerprints, so I kicked it into the open room as far as I could. It skidded across the floor and came to a stop somewhere under a stack of folding tables.

The lady at the ticket window was reading a Cosmo article when I tapped.

"Yes, can I help you?" she asked, looking up surprised.

I slipped the wallet under the window. "A man followed me into the women's restroom and tried to take pictures of me with his phone. When I saw him, he ran, dropping his wallet in the process."

Her expression turned one of worry. "Oh my." Opening the wallet and removing the ID, she asked, "Is this him?" showing me the picture.

"Yes, that's him all right. I can't hang around, but could you contact the police and file a complaint? My bus'll be here shortly."

"Yes, yes I will," she said, picking up her desk phone as I turned away.

I knew the bus would be here in less than five minutes and the closest police station was easily fifteen away.

The little girl watched me as I took the seat next to her. "So, I'm guessing you're going to Raleigh too?"

"Yes ma'am." She looked around the building and asked, "What happened to that man? The man in the hall?"

"I had a talk with him and convinced him that he should probably go somewhere else. Are you meeting someone in Raleigh?"

"My grandma."

"How 'bout I keep you company until we meet up with her?"

"I'd like that," she answered.

chapter twenty-four

Raleigh wasn't all that far from Charlotte, thirty miles or so. I'd been here many times for business and knew the area well enough. There was this one motel I'd see when passing through. It was a dive. Nasty and dirty, at least that was how it appeared from the road. It looked like one of those places that tended to attract value-minded cross-country travelers and rendezvous couples who needed a cheap bed for an hour or two. It should serve its purpose well for this trip.

I didn't pick it for its charm. I picked it for its floorplan and hopeful lack of professionalism. In the shape of a horseshoe, the parking lot was in the center with the room doors opening toward the parking. It had two levels and a long balcony encircling the top level with old iron railings in desperate need of repainting.

It was a twenty minute taxi ride from the bus station to the motel's grungy, faded green office door. The motel was just as I remembered. They hadn't surprised me with any updates or fresh paint.

"Reservation?" a guy in an old AC/DC t-shirt and shorts asked from his reclined desk chair.

"Nope," I replied, walking into the dark little office. "I need two rooms, one for myself and one for my friend coming in later tonight." In an effort to take a good ten years off of my age, I fidgeted with my backpack straps, cocked my head to the side, and smacked as though I had a wad of gum I was working on.

He leaned forward and opened a spiral ledger on the desk. "Name?" he asked and waited.

Swinging the backpack around to my side, I told him "Kaitlyn" as I dug deep down in the bottom of the pack under my few clothes, the two ammo boxes, the nine-mil, and the GPS tracker, feeling for my coin wallet, my real wallet containing my true ID and credit cards.

"For me, I'd like a room on the second level," I said, laying down Kaitlyn Cline's credit card. I held onto the ID, grasping it between my thumb and forefinger. My thumb precariously covering my birthdate.

"I got room 213."

"Ok."

"I need to see your driver's license," he said.

I held it out in front of me, keeping my thumb over the date.

His eyes went back and forth a few times from the picture on the ID to the new me standing in front of him.

He nodded, took my credit card off of his desk, and ran it through the well-worn machine, holding his hand out to catch the paper receipt as it printed out. He slid me the receipt and a pen, then asked, "And a room for your friend?"

"Yes, I have her credit card, but I don't have her ID, though. She'll be in late tonight. Is that ok? Her name is Sarah Rilley." He seemed to be buying it. Or, he just didn't care. I continued my chipper and stereotypical college-girl guise as I set the card on the desk. "She needs a room on the ground level, possibly on the other side of 213 somewhere." I waited for the request to raise suspicion.

Tilting his head, he glanced up with raised eyebrows. "Whatever floats your boat, kid. I got room 123 and 127. Both are across the parking lot from 213."

"Either one'll do."

Running the card, he said, "Tell your friend to come get the key when she gets in."

"Oh, could I possibly get the key now? I need to put some of her clothes in the room for when she gets here." I shifted weight to my right foot and crossed my arms. "She's gonna be tired when she gets here and she doesn't like walking around at night in a new place. You know," I said. "She's ... like ... prissy."

He bit his lip and shook his head saying, "Yeah, whatever."

Entering room 213 first, I knew I had some time. I ruffled up the sheets and comforter, then with care to not touch the notepad with my fingertips, I scribbled some nonsense notes on it before sticking the pen inside my pant's pocket. Fully aware that I had also left prints on the doorknob and the room key, my last step before leaving was to lather up a soapy rag. I washed the key carefully but quickly, left it on the dresser table and pulled the door shut on my way out, making sure to wipe down the knob on my exit.

  Once at the other room, the one under the name Sarah Rilley, I was happy to see that I had a direct line of sight to room 213. In picking a second floor room, I had hoped to give myself a clear visual over any cars or trucks in the center lot and also buy some valuable time.

  Dark would be coming in a few short hours and maybe, just maybe, the night would bring someone with it. Someone who'd be looking for Kaitlyn Cline. If my hunch was right, they'd come knocking on room 213, the room reserved under Kaitlyn Cline's credit card. It only made sense. Whoever was after me in Aspen had tracked my every movement either by constant surveillance or use of technology. The latter would have been much easier for them. If they were using my credit card transactions, it would have been very convenient to follow my moves without ever leaving a hotel room or coffee shop. Any simple hack into my email would have also given them the rental car receipt showing not only the make and model of the car, but the plate number as well.

It was time to let the mouse stalk the cat.

I settled into room 127 without turning on any lights. The door was shut and the curtain wide open. With the rolling desk chair placed between the room door and bed, there was a perfect line of sight to room 213's door. The chair was placed far enough away from the window that I rested in the protection of shadow.

On the bed next to my backpack lay the black magnetic plastic box containing the GPS unit.

Wait. Sit and wait.

My body barely moved for hours. But my mind raced in all directions. The fact that I shouldn't be doing this, any of this, seemed to be the resounding consensus. I was an attorney, a well-educated one at that. And very aware of every law I'd been breaking. I've sent people away to jail for committing the same crimes I'd already committed: forgery, assault, illegal firearms shipment …

I only needed to figure out who wanted me dead. What I'd actually do with that information, I still had not come to grips with yet. The educated and civilized part of me said to let the justice system works its magic with the facts. But the primal part of my being that I'd recently learned having inherited from my parents said to ... take care of it on my own.

Daylight faded into an orange thick line across the sky above the second floor of the motel roof and I'd watched maybe ten or twelve cars come and go, people walk in and out of various rooms. But not room 213 on the second floor.

Boredom and fatigue were growing strong. Was I wrong? Have I been wrong all this time? Could this all be a waste? Could've those two men in Aspen confused me or my car with someone else's? How would I ever break this to Daniel now?

I tried my best to remain awake and alert as the time ticked by. After midnight, there was a small rush of motel patrons that arrived. Each time headlights rounded the corner, I'd perk up in my chair and watch. I'd lean forward and squint my eyes following the silhouettes from the cars into the shadows of the badly-lit motel property. As soon as I lost sight of their shapes, my gaze would return to the door of room 213 waiting for someone to close in on it. Each time, my tension would be eventually released by a sliver of light coming from another room door as it'd crack open quickly, then close. I'd sit back and take a breath as my nerves returned to normalcy. Rinse and repeat. Same scenario over and over.

By 2am, I had begun to seriously doubt everything and was starting to work out the fine details of my return to Daniel, the girls, and the life of Kaitlyn Cline. I missed it. I missed it all. I missed Mattie and Olivia. I missed Daniel, and I so desperately wanted to work on becoming a better mother. A better wife. Be at home more. Actually go watch a soccer game rather than hear the updates after-the-fact as a bedside story with the girls in their pajamas and me still in dress slacks and heels. I wanted to be there for breakfast each morning and dinner each night. I wanted ... I wanted to be ... better.

I noticed the headlight beams first before it rounded the building. The beams were moving fast as the car pulled in. It was a dark sedan that rolled quickly into the center parking lot passing under the two street lights and came to a stop among the other vehicles.

I sat up.

The doors opened.

I reached behind me and unholstered the thirty-eight.

Two men stepped out of the car. They split up and walked around the parking lot, reading door numbers.

I held the thirty-eight against my thigh with my thumb on the hammer.

One of the men walked toward my room, straining his eyes.

I peddled my feet, pushing my chair further back into the shadows. I squeezed my lips shut. My nostrils flared as the air coming from my heaving lungs forced its way through, making the only audible sounds in the room.

He came closer, scanning the doors as he did. He stopped. He strained to read the brass room numbers.

The thirty-eight held tightly with both hands, muzzle pointed to the door. My eyes noticed the lock. The silver deadbolt lever was up and down. Unlocked. I had never locked the damn door.

He turned.

I heard a voice, the muffled and restrained voice of the other man. "Hey, hey," he said in a loud whisper and waved his hand to his partner who stood only fifteen feet away from my window. Watching him walk away from my room, I slid out of my chair, shoved the GPS into my back pocket and moved closer to the glass.

They crossed the parking lot, took the stairs to the second-floor balcony, and crept toward room 213.

My left hand turned the doorknob while I kept my eye on them through the window.

At the door, one of the men appeared to knock on 213. I saw the other with his back against the wall slip a long pistol out from under his shirt. He held it to his chest. Another knock.

I cracked my room door ever-so-slightly and quietly.

The man at the door of 213 squatted down in front of the lock. Eye level with it.

It took him three of my breathes to pick the lock and push the door open. They filed in. The room light came on.

I made my exit, lightly pulling my door shut behind me. Their shadows moved around the room behind the drawn curtain and I made my dash. I bolted to the dark sedan, coming to a rest behind it on my knees at the rear, directly behind the license plate. A New Jersey license plate. Without any wasted time, I reached under the rear of the car with the magnetic GPS case and felt around, finding a home for it under the rear panel next to the spare tire. A moderately loud *clank* sounded when it attached. I gave it a tug to check the adhesion. Good, good enough.

Peering to the room from around the rear of the car, I could now see inside the room through the open door. One of the men walked around looking for clues and the other stood in front of the bed. He was holding something. Studying something. Ah, my writing on the notepad. He handed it to the other.

While my note was buying me time, I dashed away from their car back into the shadows on my side of the hotel. Opening my room door at that moment would have been too dangerous. I found a corner where the brick wall made a ninety degree turn and pushed my body into it. Pulling my feet in as far as I could and squishing my shoulders into the tight corner until I could go no more, I hid.

One of the men stepped out to the balcony, lit a cigarette and leaned over the metal railing. The other made another lap inside the room before joining his buddy.

The air rushing out of my mouth in steady rhythm seemed so loud. To me anyway. Making a conscious effort, I tried to slow my heart rate by commanding my diaphragm to slow down and take heavier and longer breaths.

I saw the light turn off in room 213 and door pull shut. They walked toward the stairs.

Behind me, behind the brick wall somewhere, a door opened. Footsteps approached. I pressed even harder into the bricks.

The men on the balcony stopped and focused their attention in my direction, at the footsteps, at my corner, at me.

I held my breath. The footsteps slowed, then stopped. Literally at my flank with only inches of brick masonry separating us.

The men on the balcony still with eyes fixed on my position.

The footsteps resumed at a quickened pace. A man in a western shirt and shorts appeared from the blind spot behind the wall carrying a towel heading away from me, unaware of his surroundings. I pursed my lips, letting out a shallow sigh as he disappeared into a room four doors down.

I remained in position as the two men gradually returned to the dark sedan from New Jersey. The engine started, lights came on, and the car drove out into the night, taking my GPS along for the ride.

My body could have collapsed right there.

Safely in the room, the tightness unwound, leaving me immediately exhausted.

Deciding to check the GPS log in the morning, I slept. I literally crashed on the bed in all my clothes, curtains closed tight, and a pistol at each side of me within easy reach. I did make sure to lock the door.

chapter twenty-five

Daniel's phone rang early. He'd just woken Mattie and Olivia for school. The phone number on the screen was listed as unknown. He mumbled and set the phone down on the kitchen counter without answering.

Moments later, it rang again.

"Stupid telemarketers," he said to himself, picking it up and pressing the answer button. He answered rudely and forceful, "Yeah, what?"

"Mr. Cline. Daniel Cline?" a deep male voice asked.

"Yeah, what? This is he."

"Mr. Cline," the voice said. "I'm Scott Bertrand. I'm an agent with the FBI. Do you have a moment?"

Daniel leaned up against the counter attentive and apologetic. "Yes, I do. The number showed up as an unknown. I thought it was a junk call. I'm sorry."

"I understand. No worries. As I said, my name is Scott Bertrand. I have been assigned the missing person's case of your wife, Kaitlyn."

"Do you have anything, Mr. Bertrand?"

"Well, Mr. Cline, we don't know. I'll explain," the agent said. "Kaitlyn's credit card was swiped at a motel in Raleigh yesterday."

"In Raleigh? Here in North Carolina?"

"Yes. And by the way, you can call me Scott."

"But she went missing in Colorado."

Scott replied, "Yes, we are aware of that."

Daniel's voice reflected a tone of hope and asked, "Do you think it was her? Could she be alive?"

"It's too early to tell at this point, Mr. Cline. There's a very high possibility that someone else could have used her card."

The few seconds of hope in Daniel was squashed with Scott's remark. "Oh," was all Daniel said into the phone.

"I am sending a team out this morning to dust for prints."

"Her prints?" asked Daniel.

"Yes, her prints. We'll also collect any other prints and run them through a database just in case."

"In case of what?"

Scott paused, then answered, "In case there was foul play. Right now, anyone in possession of her items would be considered a suspect."

Daniel rubbed his hand across his forehead and said in a low voice, "I'm guessing you are meaning a suspect in her death."

"Her disappearance. And yes sir, her possible death." Scott changed the tone of the conversation quickly. "Mr. Cline, will you be available to answer some questions later today?"

"On the phone?"

"No sir. In person. At your house. It's normal protocol. May I come out this afternoon?"

Daniel, feeling unsure, answered, "Hmm, yes. Ok. After the girl's soccer practice."

"What time?"

"Five-thirty, I guess," Daniel said, pacing around the kitchen.

"Very well, I'll see you later today. Bye," Scott said before hanging up abruptly.

chapter twenty-six

The loud knock at the hotel room door brought me out of my deep sleep in a hurry. By the second knock, I was up with the thirty-eight in its holster at my lower back and the nine-mil held tightly with my thumb on the hammer.

"Hola," a lady's voice said from behind the closed door. "Hola." She knocked another time.

As I approached the door, I heard the sound of keys and saw the door knob wiggle. Hiding the nine-mil with its long silencer behind me, I unlocked the deadbolt to see a lady standing at my door with a white shirt, black pants, and a cleaning cart beside her.

"Señorita," she said. "Señorita, I need to clean room." She then repeated in Spanish, "Necesito limpiar."

I turned to the clock near the bed. 11:13am the red digital numbers showed. "Oh, I overslept. I'm so sorry. Lo Siento." As I was talking to her through the cracked door, I noticed them. They stood at the opened door of room 213. Two men in black pants, vests and caps, standing outside of the room. Movement from inside the open door indicated one more. One of the men turned to enter and the three large letters of FBI on his back let me know that there just might be another team in this game.

"Señorita," the lady said in a questioning tone as if asking me vacate at that moment.

"Lo Siento. Give me ten minutes, please?" I asked the confused woman. "Diez minutos, por favor?"

"Si," she answered, rolling her cart down the walkway to the next room.

I shut the door and went to the bathroom to rinse my face and run my fingers through my tangled hair as best I could. Leaving the bathroom, I straightened my shirt, tugged up my pants, then slid the nine-mil inside my backpack before shouldering it and taking a final peek through the window at room 213.

The men's attention was only focused on the room and the immediate area. One seemed to be dusting the knob for prints, the other on the phone, leaning up against the railing with his back to me and the third, apparently still inside.

A somber emotion took hold of me with the realization that the FBI was also looking for me. Daniel and the girls must be in fits. Not knowing if I was dead, kidnapped, or ... a runaway. Things had been so wild lately, I really hadn't taken into account that I was now a missing person. Soon. Soon this would be over and I could only hope they'd have it in their hearts to forgive me.

I slipped out of the door and made a hard right with my head down, letting my hair drape across my face to break up my outline. Keeping to the walkway, I was out of sight and around the building's corner in thirty seconds without so much as raising an eyebrow from those men investigating Kaitlyn's room.

Once away from the hotel, I walked blindly along the street of midtown Raleigh. I'd overslept, which wasn't all that surprising since I didn't get to sleep until roughly 5am. Waking my phone, I opened the GPS app. The car's tag said it was from New Jersey, and as the app loaded the coordinates of their last ping, the screen zoomed in on a dot somewhere northwest of Baltimore.

Zooming in more, the dot appeared to be on I-95 and heading … toward New Jersey. "Guess I'm goin' to Jersey," I mumbled. "… Never been there before."

chapter twenty-seven

Daniel opened the front door to a relatively young man, maybe early thirties, tall, dark hair meticulously brushed and maintained. Clean-shaven and wearing a navy blue suit, buttoned up and proper.

Agent Scott Bertrand extended his hand, "Hello, Mr. Cline, thanks for allowing me over."

Returning the handshake with a smile, Daniel said loudly over his shoulder, "Hey, girls, why don't you go find something quiet to do in your rooms." Directing his attention back to the agent, he said, "Come on in. We can sit at the table."

Scott flicked the tail of his sports coat back with both hands as he sat in the kitchen chair. He had with him no notes or papers. Sitting back in the chair with both hands palming the edge of the table, he told Daniel, "I don't mean to take up too much of your time, but I have some questions."

Daniel sat leaning forward onto the wooden surface. "Ask anything. All I want is for Kaitlyn to come back. I, well we, the girls and I, know she's alive. We can feel it. We just have no idea of what happened after the wreck."

"I understand you received a voice mail after the wreck," Scott said. "May I hear it?"

"Yeah, sure." Daniel fished his cell phone out of his pocket and fingered to the message. His face was visibly distraught before he pressed the play button.

Scott listened to the message, then asked Daniel to play it again.

"That's the last I heard from her," said Daniel.

"Ok." Scott straightened his coat sleeves. "Mr. Cline, I understand you were here in Charlotte when you got the call?"

"Yes, at the girls' soccer game. I missed the call and got the voice message a little later. I tried to call her back, then immediately called the police department there in Aspen." Daniel stared at the screen of his phone.

"Do you have any idea of how her credit card could have been used in Raleigh, Mr. Cline?"

Daniel shook his head at the question. "No, I do not."

"To your knowledge, did she have her credit cards with her in Aspen?" Scott asked.

"Yes, I'm sure of it. She'd have needed the cards to book everything, the hotel, rental car, everything. I got her purse from the scene and her small wallet isn't, I mean wasn't in there."

Scott sat upright and his gaze stiffened. "You took her purse from the scene?"

"I did."

"When?" asked Scott.

"I got it when I climbed down the side of that mountain to look at the car before they towed it up."

"The investigators allowed you to view the scene and take evidence?"

"The police were treating it as if she had just gone to get help somewhere," Daniel said. "The police told me that they searched all around and knocked on all the neighbor's houses. It wasn't treated as a crime scene, just a wrecked car."

"May I see the purse?"

"Yes." Daniel stood and went down the hall to retrieve it. "Here it is. A few of her things mixed in with broken glass and dust," he said, setting it on the table in front of Scott before returning to his seat.

Scott dug through the contents. "And you said she had a separate wallet for her cards and such?"

"Yes. It wasn't in there as I said a minute ago."

"Have you ever been to Aspen, Mr. Cline?" Scott asked.

"No. Well, yes. Soon after her wreck, I went. But I'd never been there before." Daniel shifted in his chair.

"Mr. Cline, how is you and your wife's relationship? How were things between you two?"

"Fine," answered Daniel, "she works a lot. Isn't home much."

"Have you had any recent disagreements?"

"Mr. Scott, may I ask what's being done to find Kaitlyn? These questions you're asking me seem to be a waste of your valuable time."

"Covering the basics, Mr. Cline." Scott pushed the purse to the middle of the table.

Standing and shoving his chair backwards into the wall, Daniel raised his voice. "Look here, Agent Scott, I've been trying to keep up hope for me and the girls. I call the Aspen Police and the hospital every damned day. Our family is falling apart day by day with each one that Kaitlyn isn't back being harder and harder." Daniel slammed the palms of his hands on the table and leaned in toward where Scott sat. "Every morning, those two girls in there ask me when Mom is coming home. And you know what I have to say to them, Scott?"

"No sir."

"I have to tell them that their mother is coming home any day now. I have to tell them a …"

Scott tilted his head and asked, "… tell them a what?"

In a lower voice, Daniel said, "I have to tell them a lie."

"Mr. Cline," asked Scott, "how do you know it's a lie?"

Daniel backed away from the table. "Because I'm scared. Because she hasn't been found yet. Because it's been too long. I think our time's up, Scott."

Scott slowly got up from the table and pushed his chair in. "Okay then, I may call in a couple days with some follow-up questions."

chapter twenty-eight

Rental cars are like those little plastic globes that fall out of the machine after you put in the two quarters. The plastic globes with a toy inside. You never really know what you are getting. You think you do because you can faintly see through the hazy plastic sphere, but you never really know until you open it. Like a rental car.

The pre-accident version of me made sure to get a good rental in Denver for the drive into Aspen. Nice, clean, semi-luxury. An eye-turner to serve as a reflection of me, or who I was that short time ago.

But this car, this car had personality, grunge … and an odor. The odor of a boy's sweaty gym bag. I cracked the windows as I drove north on I-95 in an effort to let the wind drag some of the smell out. North to New Jersey following my tracking device.

At last check, the GPS dot on the dark sedan from last night was still moving and already into Jersey State. I followed along blindly, not fully knowing what to expect when the dot reached its destination. My hope was for this to end as quickly as possible, but my gut told me that was very unlikely.

As day tuned into night, I could see I was gaining on the dot. They'd stopped a few times, most likely for food and gas, but they lingered at each break while my stops were quick with no time wasted. My best guess was that I was an hour or less behind them.

Well into New Jersey, the dot had stopped again. Fifteen minutes since the last ping, I kept northbound on their tail, taking the same roads and making the same turns they made.

It was nearing 9pm and I'd been driving for almost eight hours since leaving Raleigh. I was tired. I was hungry. I was nervous.

Checking the status again after three more songs on the radio, the dot hadn't moved. I hit my blinker to take the next exit and find a place to pull off. I came to a stop in an abandoned liquor store parking lot right off of the exit ramp. My headlights brushed across the old building. Broken windows, trash strewn about, and tall weeds growing up through the cracks in the pavement.

I took a moment to stretch and crack my back before zooming into the stationary dot on my phone screen. Montville, New Jersey. Zooming in closer. 436

Dover Circle, Montville, New Jersey. A residential address, or so it seemed. Thirty-four minutes from where I sat.

I needed to see this place, get an idea of what it is, who might live there. Although, the dark of night was not the best time. My headlights would raise suspicion and ambling around on foot in the dark at an unknown location was not a good idea either.

Deciding to wait until morning would be best, I turned off the ignition, locked the doors, and reclined the seat back as far as it would go. Before dozing off, I tucked the thirty-eight comfortably underneath my thigh.

Morning came like a flash, a flash of sunlight as it blasted through the windshield. Once that big orange ball of fury rose above the tree-line over the top of the old liquor store, my windshield became a prism almost intentionally directing the light onto my closed eyes.

Sitting up, I checked my surroundings and slid the thirty-eight into its holster at my lower back. Then, waking my cell phone, I found the GPS dot to still be at the same address. The dot's history, though, from overnight, showed that it had traveled again after midnight and returned to the address just after seven-thirty this morning.

Still too early to call Monica about the address, I let the seat spring back upright and turned the ignition key.

The car still stunk and I was beginning to stink. My clothes needed a wash and I needed a shower. To make matters somewhat worse, the air blowing from the a/c vent only magnified each of the odors.

Thirty-two minutes to my destination driving northwest on Highway 24. At least that was what the voice on the phone told me.

chapter twenty-nine

"*Five minutes from your destination,*" the phone narrated. I was getting closer and the closer I got, the more the rental car and I stood out. There are nice neighborhoods and there are rich neighborhoods. I'd seen them all, or so I'd thought.

This place. This place nearly caused my jaw to drop. Expansive plots of land with manicured lawns all a few acres in size. The scattered patches of trees in each of the huge yards helped to give the country club feel to each estate. The roads within the subdivision curved and flowed beautifully, not like the choppy gridded pattern streets of even the richest of areas I'd been in before.

Wrought-iron fencing traced the curbside serpentine outline of the estates with massive brick structures every hundred feet or so along the iron fences.

I slowed in awe.

At each driveway stood another massive brick foundation that held a metal mailbox cemented inside with a keypad and speaker facing the driveway. Behind those, to serve as both a physical and social barrier, stood ornate iron gates that opened up in the middle, swinging away to each side. Some had letters welded on them, some were simply blank, anonymous and elite. This was a neighborhood where normal people were not to be without invitation and it was made apparently obvious.

Set far back away from the road on each of the estates, the actual homes appeared as pure fiction. The sizes of them, even from the road distance, just didn't seem believable. Three or four stories of glass windows stood above the perfect green grass yards. Wrap-around decks divided the overall height into two sections and patio furniture with big table umbrellas decorated some of the decks.

I chuckled to myself thinking about how high-class I used to feel in my Mercedes when people would notice and give me that second glance. This was true high-class.

"You are three-hundred feet from your destination," my phone told me. I slowed the car more, squinting my eyes to see the brass numbers screwed to the brick mailbox foundation. 436.

There was no home visible. Passing the driveway, I stopped on the street. The black asphalt driveway curved away to the right from the closed gate into a batch of trees and then swept back left behind them. Daylight could be seen through those trees giving way to a faint green hue of what I imagined to be the very private yard.

I double-checked the dot on the GPS app. Yep, the dark sedan from the hotel was parked back there, somewhere, behind that gate.

Replaying my last talk with Dad in my mind, I have to admit, if this *is* one of Matteo Bianchi's rivals in the drug business, then business must be good. Putting the car in gear, I drive off so not to arouse suspicion.

At a truck stop diner off of the interstate just out of Montville city limits and only a few miles, but a world away from the neighborhood, a waitress from three generations past wearing a checkered apron slid my breakfast plate in front of me. "Anything else I can get you, dear?" she asked.

"No thanks," I replied. Still too early to call Monica and Elmore, I faded into a daze eating the pancakes slowly and mindlessly.

"Ok, just call me if you need anything. My name's Shirley," the waitress said before turning away.

I'd find out whose mansion that was shortly. But how could I be certain that whoever lived behind those gates was the person who wanted me gone. I must be one hundred percent correct. I could not be wrong. How though? The question tumbled around in my head.

Time had gotten away from me sitting there in the sticky, vinyl covered booth. I had my elbows on the table and my hands cradling my face when the waitress slipped the bill on the table, purposely touching my arm with it. "Are you a'right, little lady?" she asked. "You're lookin' like you got a lot goin' on in that head a'yours."

"Oh, I'm sorry," I answered, "just thinking about things."

"Like what?" Shirley asked, looking as if she'd stepped right out of an article of Life Magazine from the early nineteen-sixties. Behind her apron, she wore a light pink shirt with a white collar. A head of curly red hair was pulled up into a ponytail and bright red lipstick with heavy mascara drew attention away from her years of wrinkles.

"Trying to figure out how get some information, that's all." I'd no intention to be rude, though I couldn't quite go into detail either.

The diner was nearly empty and I could tell that this lady was eager to chat. Kinda like a hairdresser. Once you get in that chair, you're stuck there. She seemed like that.

Shirley plopped down in the booth across from me and reached out, touching my arms. "Is your problem with a boy?"

I smiled at the fact that she thought I was a young, distraught lover. Her sincerity was heartwarming. I answered the truth, "Yes, a boy," guessing that Matteo's rival would most likely be male.

"Oh dear, do you feel your man is cheating?" she asked.

Shaking my head, I answered, "I don't know."

She leaned forward with her face near the middle of the table, only a few inches from my own, as she whispered, "You know what you need to do?"

"No, what's that?"

She continued, "You call up that boy and you tell him to meet you face to face. Then you ask him. His eyes'll tell you the truth even if his words don't." She slapped the table lightly with the palms of her hands and took my empty plate with her as she left the booth saying, "You do that, take my word on it."

"Thanks for the talk," I told her as she walked off. "I think I'll do just what you said."

"Hello, Kait," Monica answered in such a friendly tone that anyone would have thought we'd have been coworkers for years. "What can I help you with this morning?"

"Hi, Monica, I need some information."

I couldn't see her face, but it sounded like she smiled. "Sure, I'll do what I can. What are you needing?"

"I need to know the name of the owner and a phone number for an address," I said.

"Ok, give me the address," chirped Monica. "I'm ready."

"436 Dover Circle, Montville, New Jersey," I recited slowly. "Do you think you can get that?"

"We shall see. The owner should be easy. Phone number, maybe, maybe not. I'll call you as soon as I have something."

"That's fine, I'm just driving around this city checking out the sights."

As soon as I hung up with her, I dialed Dad.

"Kait, I've been worried about you," he said the moment he picked up the phone. "Any news?"

"Actually, yes. I'm getting close to finding out a name. Get this, the trail brought me to New Jersey."

"Wow, really?"

"Yeah, I can explain the details later. I'm waiting on a homeowner's name and possible phone number from Elmore's office."

Dad's wheelchair squeaked some as he rolled around. "Good. Are you going to contact the police?"

"No. Not yet. I don't know. I've got one more step to be sure I'm onto the right person."

"Well, be careful," he said. "Why don't you go ahead and get you some leather driving gloves."

"Driving gloves?"

"Yes, I've always like the driving gloves for jobs better than the other alternatives. Leaves no fingerprints and still very sensitive on the trigger finger."

"Will do," I said.

"If you have to handle anything on your own, get in and get out. Don't waste any time thinking about things. Do your thinking beforehand."

It was still such a shock to hear my warm and loving dad talk like that with such ease. "Oh, and Dad…" I wanted to tell him about seeing the FBI search the hotel room in Raleigh. But…

"What?"

I paused a second and decided against it, "Never mind."

"Ok then," he said. "You be careful and …"

"Yes, Dad?"

He cleared his throat and lowered his voice. "I love you."

He'd never been one for emotions and I knew those simple words were sincere, and at the same time, a bit hard for him to say. I'd come to learn that some of the toughest people in this world are also the most emotional. They tended to hide it well and anything that caused an outward display of that emotion was difficult, including saying three little words.

I replied, "I love you too, Dad. We'll talk later. Bye."

An hour later, my phone rang. I'd parked at a shopping mall and was watching customers go in and out, waiting for the call. I answered, "Did you find anything?"

"Yes," said Monica, "I'm so sorry it took some time. I had to do lots of research since the home is owned by an LLC. Are you ready?"

I sat up in the seat. All of sudden very nervous. Her next few words would help me put an end to this, once and for all. "Go ahead. I don't have anything to write with, but I'll try to remember."

"I'll tell you first and I'll text the details to you after we hang up. Is that ok?"

"Sure." I was actually trembling.

"Just be sure to delete my text as soon as you can."

"Ok."

"The home at the address you gave me, 436 Dover Circle, is owned by Beaches Casinos LLC. Here is what took me so long, I had to figure out who was in charge of that LLC. I kept coming across various CFOs and CEOs. Finally, I found a break in the DMV records by cross-referencing cars registered to that address as well."

"Yes?" I said, leaning all the way up against the steering wheel."

Monica continued, "I'm certain with ninety percent accuracy that a Jeff Mitchell owns that residence."

The name Jeff Mitchell rang in my head. I'd never heard of that name before, but it stuck. It was implanted as the words came through the phone. "Were you able to determine a phone number?"

"I was," she answered. "But only a land line. I was not able to find any cell phone numbers linked the name Jeff Mitchell or the LLC."

Monica slowly told me the phone number twice and promised to text it upon our disconnect.

Jeff Mitchell. Could that be the name of who wanted me dead? Tried to kill me in Aspen? Is this guy a drug trafficker? A rival of Matteo Bianchi? Is this guy really a casino owner? Is the casino a cover for getting drug money into the system?

The phone shook in my quivering hand as I waited for the text message. *Ding,* the phone chimed. I stared at the phone number as if it were the most important thing in my world. The phone *dinged* again with another message. Monica had also sent an image. An image of Jeff Mitchell. It was one of those business-type headshots like you'd see hanging on the wall in some boardroom. I studied his face. The picture was obviously an old one, but it didn't matter. Looking into his dark brown eyes on my phone screen, I could see right through him. The picture showed a man of stature and importance. One with an intentional five-o'clock shadow for a beard and somewhat short dark brown hair. After a few seconds, the screen began to fade. I touched it lightly to make the image appear again and sat there with my eyes glued to it as if waiting for something more. As if waiting for some instruction of what to do next.

Just the thought of making the call was terrifying.

I can do this, I thought to myself. *I have to do this. It'll all be over soon. One way or another.* I knew deep down what my next steps were. And ... if those steps went as planned, I'd be back in Charlotte very soon explaining to Daniel how I ended up with a bad haircut and dye job after the wreck.

chapter thirty

Inside the mall at a pay phone in a secluded corner near the restrooms, my hand gripped the receiver tightly. I was scared. Petrified. I closed my eyes, dropped the final coin and then put the phone to my ear.

"Hello, how may I help you?" a young lady's voice greeted.

I froze.

"Hello," the lady repeated. "Hello, how can I help you?"

Barely able to get the words out, I asked her, "May I speak with Jeff Mitchell?" I took the chance of saying the name, figuring if he wasn't the owner, she'd surely say so or say that he didn't live there or whatever.

Silence.

"May I ask who's calling please?"

My entire body tingled with anxiety as I answered her question. "Kaitlyn Cline. Tell him that Kaitlyn Cline is calling from McGillis and Associates Law Firm."

"Yes, one moment," she said before the *bump* sound of the phone as it was laid down on something hard, like a desk, I suppose.

Chills went up and down my spine as I listened for any sound. After a short while, I could hear mumbling in the distance and then footsteps. Heavy footsteps. Those of a large person. Someone picked up. "Hello, this is Jeff." The voice matched the large footsteps. A big man. A confident man. A man who most likely only came to the phone because of the name I gave. "Who is this again?" he asked.

"Hi, Mr. Mitchell, this is Kaitlyn Cline from McGillis and Associates Law Firm. We've never met."

He interrupted me, "Then why are you calling me?"

Trying to keep the consistent naive tone going, I replied, "Mr. Mitchell, I am an attorney working on the case of Phillip Bianchi, Matteo Bianchi's nephew. I'd like to ask some questions regarding your relationship with Mr. Matteo."

"What makes you feel that I know him?"

Thinking quickly, I came up with an answer that made sense in the moment and said, "I saw your name mentioned within some documents. I'm sure it's nothing, but it'd clear up things if we could meet in person."

"When?" he was getting frustrated and it was apparent.

"Well, Mr. Mitchell, I am in the area today regarding other business. We could meet later this evening, just outside of Montville at the Quality Inn. I plan to stay there for the night."

"What time?"

"Oh, I'd say about nine-thirty tonight. I should be settled in by then," I waited through the silence on his end of the line, fully expecting him to hang up on me.

"Sure, I'll swing by. See you then."

I purposely did not mention anything about a room number or calling to give him one. If I was correct, he'd know the room number as soon as the counter clerk entered my old credit card.

Hanging up, I blended into the steady traffic of shoppers as they paraded past the shop windows. "Ok Kait, let's go try on some driving gloves," I told myself.

chapter thirty-one

Jeff hung up the phone in the living room and stood there. Crossing his arms, he stared out of the front door window. Not looking at anything in particular, only letting his mind wrap around the fact that Kaitlyn Cline just called him. The same Kaitlyn Cline that Antonio's men were supposed to have taken care of.

The maid walked back into the living room and asked, "Mr. Jeff, is everything ok?"

"It will be soon," said Jeff, turning to go into his office. Slamming the door behind him, he paced in front of his custom-made metal and wood desk. An open door that led out to the deck overlooked the yard and let in a draft of fresh air.

Jeff finally calmed down enough to stand in the doorway and retrieve his cell phone from his jeans pocket. Scrolling through the contact list, his thumb tapped on a number labeled as Unknown.

"Get me Antonio," he forcefully said as soon as someone picked up on the other line. "Now!" While waiting, he nervously tapped his foot against the doorjamb.

"Antonio, we've got an issue," Jeff said into the cell phone. "Two nights ago, I got a notification that the lady lawyer's card was used in Raleigh. Thinking it was just a fluke deal with a stolen card, I sent two of my men down there to check on things. And guess what? Only five minutes ago, she fuckin' called me on my house phone."

Jeff listened, shifting his weight to the other side of the door. Regaining his turn to talk, he said, "I just got off of the phone with her. She's obviously alive and well. What do you take me for, Antonio?" Jeff shouted into the speaker. "Look, you got me into this and I trusted you to complete things on your end. I provided the fuckin' information and your guys were supposed to take care of the ground work."

Jeff stepped inside and began pacing again with the phone still to his ear. "You fucked up, Antonio. I'll get this taken care of. But you fucked up. And if I even remotely think that you are up to something, I'll come down there and take care of you too."

Hanging up, he tossed the phone into a nearby chair and went out of the door onto the deck. From the second level deck, one could see over the flawless lawn and into a small grove of trees fifty yards away. Jeff's home was the most private and largest in the neighborhood. He could see no other homes and no one could see his.

Jeff walked back and forth on the deck near the metal railing with his arms crossed. The bright sunlight washing across the wood planks. His mind was running at full speed.

"Carla!" he yelled. "Carla!"

The maid quickly entered through the office door and out onto the deck. "Yes sir?"

"Figure out where Max and Carlos are and get them out here."

"Yes sir," she said, disappearing through the doors.

Minutes later, the two requested men filed out to the deck cautiously. Both in tan slacks with short-sleeved button up shirts, looking much more professional than Jeff's jeans and wrinkled shirt. They'd been warned of Jeff's mood and they knew his temper. "You need us?" one of them questioned apprehensively.

Jeff faced them. "Remember the trip to Raleigh?"

"Yes," the taller one answered.

"Remember I had you look for a specific person? A lady named Kaitlyn Cline."

"Yes sir, but there was no sign of her. There was only that note with a bunch of gibberish on it."

Jeff rubbed the back of his neck. "Carlos," Jeff told the taller one. "She'll be here in Jersey tonight."

Both men's eyes jumped at the news, knowing the order that was coming next.

"Go to the Quality Inn on the interstate tonight. Show up about ten."

"Ok?" Carlos questioned.

"And finish her," Jeff mumbled. "I'll call you with the room number once she checks in."

The men, waiting for more orders, didn't move.

"Go." Jeff said. "Find something to occupy yourselves until tonight. Get outta my face." Resting his elbows on the railing, he stared out over his property.

chapter thirty-two

I spent the rest of the day driving around the mid-sized town of Montville. It was a nice and quiet place. I could live here. Not in Jeff Mitchell's neighborhood, but I could see my family in some of the less opulent ones.

Five o'clock found me back at the same diner near the interstate that I'd visited earlier in the morning. Walking in, I wondered to myself why I'd decided to return when there were so many other eateries around. Maybe it was the human nature of striving for familiarity. A little bit of the sameness. We are creatures of habit no matter how hard we try to fight it or disagree.

Maybe my subconscious needed a familiar setting for the first time in … I don't even know how many days. I've lost count. Deep down, maybe I hoped to see the friendly face of Shirley again. I knew that was doubtful, though, since she'd already worked the morning shift.

I settled into a different booth, on the opposite end of the building than before. My was back toward the kitchen and I made sure to face the entrance. Picking up the stiff laminated menu, I read through the dishes even though I had made my mind up on a burger as soon as I'd entered. I smelled fries. Or, fried something. Anyway, that initial smell made me hungry for fries and a burger.

"Now lookie here," she said, pushing through the swinging door carrying a basket of replacement ketchup bottles. Shirley walked past me, patting me on the shoulder with her free hand. "I'll be right with you."

"No hurry," I said with a smile. Something about her. She was just infectious, I guess. One of those people who everyone seemed to like. Or was it just me? Was it the magnetic appeal of her personality? Or the motherly way she talked with me earlier? Were my emotions striving to catch a small glimpse into a life I'd missed out on? A simple mother-daughter talk.

She dropped into the booth across from me with her appearance reminding me again of a time gone by. "Well?" she asked.

"Well what?"

Tilting her head, she looked at me like I was intentionally holding something back. "The boy. Did you call him? Did you meet him face to face?"

"I did call him."

"And?" she asked with shrug of her shoulders.

"I'm supposed to meet up with him this evening," I replied.

The bell on the door rang as a lady about my age walked in alone. Shorter than myself, long blonde hair, light skin, and dressed in simple jean shorts and a white t-shirt. A very attractive lady. I only noticed her because the diner was so dead. I said to Shirley, "You may need to help that lady."

"Oh, I'll get to her in just a quick second." Shirley reached across the table and took my right hand, clasped both of her hands around mine and squeezed tight. "That's good that you're gonna meet up with that boy. That's good. You make sure and ask the questions you need answers to. And if those answers are not what you want to hear, you straighten up like a strong woman and you put that young man behind you. You hear me?"

"I hear you."

"You move on with your life. Be strong," she said, finally letting loose of my hand. "Now, what can I get you to eat?"

chapter thirty-three

I laid my credit card on the counter of the Quality Inn just before 9pm and showed the man my ID.

"Hmm," said the middle-aged man with salt and pepper hair, grinning in a perverted way after eyeing the picture on the ID. He then looked me up and down. "You've changed a lot, Miss Kaitlyn Cline. For the good, I might add. You don't even look like the same person."

Keeping my cool, I only asked, "You got a room in the back?"

He winked and said, "I sure do. You working tonight?"

Realizing what he was implying, I answered, "Maybe."

"How many?" he asked as he ran my card through the machine.

I quickly yanked the card out of his nasty fingers and said, "My business. Not yours. Gimme the key card, please?"

He teased me by very slowly handing the key card over. "Room 146. Go through that hall," he said, pointing to my left. "Out the door and around to the right."

Walking down the hall, I slipped on my new leather driving gloves.

The room was big and poorly lit. Two queen sized beds were against the wall to the right, a long counter with a TV on it to the left and the bathroom at end to the right. In the very back left corner was a tall and narrow wooden wardrobe with two doors that opened from the center.

I closed the door, purposely leaving the deadbolt unlocked. Letting my mind formulate a plan or somewhat of a plan, I went to the wardrobe and swung open the doors. It was an open box with a clothes bar at the top. Walking back to the front of the room near the door, I turned on one lamp and flipped the main light off.

Good.

The back left corner where the wardrobe stood was nearly black from the darkness.

Perfect. Next.

At the furthest bed from the door, I took two of the extra pillows and stuffed them underneath the covers to resemble myself sleeping. It wasn't the greatest, but in the darkness of the room, it'd pass.

It was 9:17. I told Jeff to meet me at 9:30.

Time to wait.

Taking the nine millimeter out of my backpack, I made sure the clip was in good and the silencer on tight. I tossed the backpack onto the first of the two beds and returned to the wardrobe where I worked myself inside into the floor of it and sat cross-legged, half-encased in the furniture piece.

From where I sat, I could see the door clearly. The one lamp was dim, its incandescent bulb created a weak yellow glow to the front of the room. With the light source near the door, it would create a level of night-blindness for anyone trying to focus into the rest of the room.

I truly did not expect Jeff himself to show. I was betting my life on it. But if he did. I didn't know … I hadn't given that much thought.

I'd have to digress on what I told him on the phone, about seeing his name mentioned in papers while going through evidence for the Philip Bianchi case. I'd invite him in. I'd be polite. And I'd keep myself at the ready. I had to realize that he could always try to finish the job himself. *If he does come, keep plenty of distance, and stay alert,* I thought. I'd finally be face to face with the man who went to great lengths to have me killed on that mountain outside of Aspen. I couldn't let my guard down because I didn't know his training or experience. I didn't come this far to have my girls hear that I'd been killed in some hotel room where the clerk thought I was turning tricks.

9:37.

He isn't going to show.

Shit, what next?

It had to be him. My gut felt it.

The sedan. The GPS tracker. It just had to be him.

9:39.

He isn't going to show.

My legs were cramping up. My hands were getting sweaty inside the leather driving gloves. And I was beginning to second-guess everything.

9:41.

Watching the digital clock between the two beds was torture.

9:42.

The door handle jiggled lightly.

I heard a key card slide into the electronic slot.

The latch clicked.

My fingers tightened up around the pistol grip.

I held my breath.

The door handle rotated all the way down.

My thumb pulled back my pistol's hammer.

In one quick instant, the door flung open violently and two men stepped in with handguns drawn. They were silhouettes in the single lamp's glow. Their attention went straight to the bed with the dummy pillows under the covers. I caught a glimpse of their weapons, like mine, long pistols with silencers.

Flashes of light illuminated the room as I heard the light *tap* sounds of each round as they fired into the comforter. Three, four, five …

The white bedsheets jumped with each bullet.

My mind went blank. The room seemed to go silent as I lifted my nine-mil toward the bright flashes that were still coming from their muzzles. Letting my instincts take over, I fired into the chest of the guy on the left and without hesitation, my sights moved to man number two where I fired again into the widest part of the upper torso I could see in the moment.

The flashes ceased.

Two heavy *thuds*.

All quiet.

I stood up from my low perch seeing that the first man fell near the bed. His face hidden by the corner, but unmoving. He was a wearing a grey t-shirt and the dark liquid had already begun to cover his entire midsection. His lifeless hand still grasped the pistol as it lay on the carpet.

The second man had fallen back into the wall near the door. Blood smears on it showed where he slid down before coming to a rest on the floor with his upper body barely upright, supported by the wall. His eyes were focused on me as I took small steps toward him. His chest heaved in and out. A puddle of blood was beginning to form under him. My shot was good, but not good enough.

The darkened room and the bright flashes from their pistols had made it hard to be accurate.

His pistol had fallen just out of reach. I stood over him with my weapon held loosely in my right hand. He began to mouth something. A whisper.

I pointed the nine at his head.

Another whisper. "Don't. Please," he said in a pained low tone.

The hammer on the nine was still cocked from the two rounds I fired only seconds ago.

"Don't. You don't have to," he said.

"I know I don't have to, mister," I told him. "It's a choice. You made the choice to work for Jeff. You made the choice to come here tonight."

"Don't," he pleaded.

"We all make choices," I said and then I pulled the trigger one last time. His head flung back with the shot. Blood splattered all over the wall directly behind him and his eyes glazed over immediately.

The only sound in the room was my breathing. The adrenaline faded away in an instant. Knowing that I needed to get out very soon, I reached down and felt his pockets for a cell phone. Upon finding it, I shoved it into my cargo pants, stepped over their bodies and grabbed my backpack off of the bed, sliding the nine-mil inside.

I carefully tugged the door shut as I walked out of the room.

chapter thirty-four

I don't even remember getting in the rental car and driving away from the Quality Inn. It was all a blur. Just before 11pm, I found a small neighborhood play area and pulled into a parking spot. With the reality hitting me, I began to shake. I replayed over and over in my head what happened in that room.

    I needed fresh air and I needed to walk around and process things. Before stepping out of the car, I felt for the thirty-eight to ensure it was still in place.

    Once the echo from me shutting the car door faded into silence, I walked to a small bench near the swingset. Everything in the park appeared as vague shadows. Through the trees above, the moon sent its filtered light down. There were no true colors on the well-worn earth around me, only the unsaturated, darkened hues where the colors once were before the sun had set on this unforgettable night. The faint outlines from the tree limbs spiderwebbed across the ground, barely touching the tips of my shoes, inviting me into their world.

I leaned forward, placing my elbows on my thighs with the palms of my hands cradling my cheeks as if I were a lonely child on a schoolyard.

It was done.

There was no going back now.

I'd done it.

I'd trained for it.

And unknowingly, I'd been training for it since childhood.

I'd done it. I'd taken a life … two of them to be exact. In only mere seconds.

Dad had taught me so much. He taught me what to expect. He taught me the techniques I'd need to defend myself. He taught me about my reactions and mental work. But he didn't teach me about how it would feel. He never went into the emotions I'd be going through after the fact.

Dad made it sound so easy. Pull a trigger and walk away. No mention about what it looked like to watch the last bit of life drift out of someone's eyes. Listening to the last huff of air leave their mouths without ever taking in another. The silence after the storm.

Maybe each one gets easier. Maybe each one becomes more uniform, habitual, and … professional.

Maybe.

But I didn't plan to find out. One more and I was done. Once Jeff Mitchell had paid the ultimate price, then I'd be back at 410 Bowmer Lane. Back to Daniel, Mattie, and Olivia. Back to a normal life. A better life with less time at the office and more time at home.

I began to daydream with my thoughts going to my arms wrapped around Daniel each morning. I'd help him make breakfast and we could all sit at the table and discuss the day's plans. I could drop the girls off at school and hear them tell me "Bye. I love you, Mom" as I watched them run off toward the school doors. A normal life.

Sitting on that bench thinking, I started to cry. All those things I yearned for, I'd had at the tip of my fingers all along. I'd just ignored them and chose a different path day after day until it became the norm. I was still *Mom*, but I wasn't part of the family anymore. I hadn't been in a long time. Daniel picked up each piece of life that I dropped so perfectly and effortlessly that I never even noticed. He never complained, never fussed. He'd simply say, "I'll take care of it." And he did, allowing me to become an outsider looking in. Looking into a life that I was once part of.

Come to think of it, it had been three years since I'd brought the girls trick or treating. Daniel even did their costumes. I only saw them because he texted me a picture.

Letting my head fall into my lap on crossed arms, I wept like I hadn't wept since standing over my mother's coffin as a girl.

Exhaustion took over. Lying down, I let myself relax before eventually falling asleep on a random park bench under the New Jersey moonlight.

A light tap on my shoulder woke me in an instant. My eyes opened and at the same time, my hand went behind my back and grasped the three-eighty in its holster.

Blinking a few times, my vision cleared to see a dark blue uniform standing over me. The silver badge on his shirt reflected brightly in the early-morning sunlight. I slowly let my fingers ease off of the pistol.

"Miss," he said. "Miss, are you ok?"

"Oh, yes. Yes, I'm fine," I said, sitting up. "I'm sorry, I know I shouldn't have fallen asleep here."

"You're right, Miss. If you need a shelter, there is one on Third and Vine."

I rubbed my eyes and stretched with the previous night being a distant memory, almost.

chapter thirty-five

Daniel recognized the car as soon as he made the corner. Agent Scott Bertrand's car was parked on the road in front of the house and he was leaning up against the door of it, looking at his phone. He gave a professional smile, watching Daniel pull into the driveway.

"Girls, go on inside," Daniel told Mattie and Olivia as they hopped out of the car. "I'll be in shortly."

Scott approached Daniel with hand outstretched. "Mr. Cline, may I bother you again?"

"For what?" Daniel asked. His eyes went to Scott's open hand, but he failed to accept. "You here to ask me more leading questions? Insinuate that I've got something to do with Kaitlyn's disappearance?"

"Mr. Cline," said Scott, "I have to cover all bases like I explained before. I truly do apologize for any discomfort."

Daniel crossed his arms and widened his stance. "So, I'm guessing you have no new information if you're here interrogating me again?"

"On the contrary, Mr. Cline." Scott motioned to the house. "May we go sit down and talk?"

Daniel let his gaze wander to some kids playing down the street. After some silence, he said, "Sure." Leading the way inside, Daniel pointed Scott to the same chair as before at the kitchen table.

"Not to waste any of your time, I'll get to the point," Scott said.

"Please do."

The agent wiggled around in the chair getting situated, laid his arms on the table and leaned forward toward where Daniel sat. "I'll have to ask some hard questions again."

"Thanks for the warning. Go on."

"Kaitlyn's credit card was used another time last night. This time in New Jersey." Scott paused. He carefully studied Daniel's reaction. "It was used at a hotel off of the interstate. Her ID was also verified by the clerk."

"Was it her?"

"The hotel clerk said the height, weight, and ethnicity matched." Scott intertwined his fingers in front of him on the table. "But he said the lady who used it looked quite different in appearance."

"How so?"

"The clerk said that the person who rented the room looked younger with black hair. He referred her as a goth kid," Scott said, looking around the room. "Maybe college age."

"What do you think?" asked Daniel. "Do you think it was Kaitlyn?"

Scott's eyebrows raised slightly as he answered, "Don't know. I just don't know."

"You don't know. You said that in an odd way. What do you mean exactly?"

Leaning back into his chair and letting his arms fall into his lap, Scott took a breath. "If it was her, then I'm really worried about what she could be wrapped up in."

"You'll need to explain," Daniel said.

"Because of what my field agents found inside the room."

"And?"

"There were two bodies inside her room. Both men, both armed, both shot in the chest and one was finished off with a head shot." Watching Daniel's reaction again, Scott continued, "We honestly feel that it was an assassination attempt that went very wrong for the two men due to the evidence obtained in the room."

Daniel's hand rose to cover his mouth in disbelief. "An assassination attempt," he repeated. He then asked, "But no sign of Kaitlyn? No fingerprints? DNA? Anything?"

Shaking his head, Scott replied, "No. No fingerprints of hers. And as for DNA, that isn't so simple. There are hundreds if not thousands of various hairs and skin cells on a hotel room floor. The cleaning crew does vacuum, but they use that same vacuum cleaner in every one of those rooms. Hair strands can get cleaned up or they may simply get spread around from room to room."

Daniel looked at Scott dumbfounded, not believing what he was hearing. "So, someone has Kaitlyn's cards and ID running around killing people? This is crazy."

"Mr. Cline," Scott asked without expression, "do you know if Kaitlyn was in any kind of trouble? Owed money to anyone? Owed favors? Anything?"

"No, of course not. You don't think she had anything to do with killing those men, do you?" Daniel leaned back and ran his finger through his hair.

"My gut tells me no. I don't believe she had anything to do with the killings, but if there's a slight chance that she was the one who rented that room, then we need to dig harder. She is either in some sort of trouble or …"

"Or what?" asked Daniel.

"Or, she's mixed up in something."

Daniel shook his head side to side in silence.

Scott readjusted his posture in the chair. "Mr. Cline, what do you know of Kaitlyn's past? We know some of the obvious, but would you please share some more of your wife's history?"

"Oh shoot, I don't have much, honestly," Daniel said. "We met in the later years of college. She was a Junior and I was a Senior. She had no hobbies, nor did I when we met. We were both focused on classes and each other."

"What about her family?"

"She grew up with her father in Phoenix, Arizona through childhood. He's in a wheelchair now."

"What happened?"

Daniel looked to the cabinets thinking. "If I remember right, it was a gas leak that caused it."

"A gas leak?"

"Yeah, a gas leak that caused the explosion. After months of treatment, he's now bound to a chair and lives in New Mexico. We haven't seen him in a couple years. I've only been to his house one time. He used to fly out here once a year but Kaitlyn kinda grew away from him, I guess. I never asked."

Scott was taking mental notes. "No mother around?"

"No, her mother was killed when Kaitlyn was a child."

"Do you know how?" asked Scott.

"A robbery, I believe. It was a filling station or some other kind of walk-in convenience store. Kaitlyn never really talked about it. It was just she and her dad from about fifth grade on."

chapter thirty-six

From an empty parking lot just after noon, I sat in the car with the phone I took from the man in the hotel room. The one who lived long enough to beg. Going through his recent call list, I studied the times and the consistencies of the calls. After a few minutes, I settled in on two numbers. One of them had more connections during daytime hours while the other number was called more after 5pm and again later in the evenings. Taking a wild guess, I judged that number to be a possible lady friend and I placed my bet on the first number.

I'd found it.

Well, I'd hoped.

I'd spoken with Jeff once and I would recognize his voice if he answered. What was I going to say to him? That, I didn't know. Deciding to just *wing* it, I pressed the number on the dead guy's phone.

My heart raced with the anticipation.

Ringing ... ringing ... ringing ... "Hey, where the hell are you two?" the voice yelled into the phone.

It startled me and my mind went blank for a moment. I didn't simply forget what I was going to say, I had gone into the call without a plan and I was, all of a sudden, speechless.

"You there? Where the fuck are you?" the voice yelled. Hearing it the second time, I was positive that the voice did belong to Jeff.

"Jeff," I said calmly into the phone.

"Who the fuck is this?"

"Hi, Jeff," I said. "This is Kaitlyn Cline."

Jeff's end of the line went quiet. He was obviously confused and didn't know what to say next. He knew the phone belonged to one of his men. And he knew that I should be dead. Why would I be calling him from his own guy's phone? I could tell through the silence he was thinking something along those lines.

"Jeff, your men failed."

There was no response.

I continued, "Jeff, your men failed. Jeff, you failed. Your men are dead now."

Finally, he came unhinged. "You bitch. How'd you get Max's phone? Where's Max?"

Still speaking calmly, I said, "Oh, that was his name. I'm sorry, we didn't exchange names when he was begging me not to end him. To answer your question, though, he's no longer with us, Jeff."

"You're lying, bitch. There's no way."

"There's no way ... what, Jeff? Is there no way little ol' me could'a killed Max and his friend?" The conversation had turned in my favor. Jeff was lost. He didn't know what was true and what wasn't. "Jeff?"

There was no response.

"Hey, Jeff?" I repeated.

"What?"

"Jeff, you've made a mistake. You've made a deadly mistake," I said. "A very deadly mistake."

The phone then erupted with shouts and profanities. Having to hold the speaker a couple inches away from my ear, I listened to him blurt out how he was going to make sure I ended up dead and floating in some river of which I didn't know the name of. But he must have. He explained to me that my body would be so fucked up that I'd be unrecognizable. Something about fish eating me and other stuff.

He was still carrying on when I pressed the button to disconnect, opened the car door, and dropped Max's phone onto the asphalt.

Dad once told me that if you stir up a hornet's nest, you have to wait until the hornets settle down before doing anything else. I'd stirred up Jeff's nest. I had to. The call to him confirmed everything.

I decided to take a drive out to the beach for a day or so and let Jeff's blood pressure return to normal. In order to finish him, I needed him to be predictable and back into some sort of routine. It was simply too dangerous at the moment, he'd be expecting me.

chapter thirty-seven

Jeff sat in his desk chair, leaning back. Talking to himself aloud, he said, "One simple job. One stupid fuckin' lawyer bitch. All Antonio's idea." He rubbed the palm of his hand over the stubble on his chin, thinking.

Gazing blindly across the top of his desk and out of the big windows to the yard and trees surrounding his estate, Jeff's eyes were focused on nothing in particular. He pulled the Marlboro Reds pack out of his shirt pocket, flipped open the lid, carefully removed one cig out. His movements were all by habit and his eyes were still on the estate when he set the butt of the cigarette onto his bottom lip and closed the pack with his left hand.

The unlit Marlboro dangled loosely between his lips, held in place only by the moisture of his skin.

Time passed with no movement from him. He was man of action and few mistakes. He'd made a successful business from nothing by not messing up. He knew the importance of perfection and precision and he had to agree with that lady lawyer, he had made a big mistake. Deadly ... maybe. It proved to be deadly for Max and Carlos.

Still rocked back in his desk chair, he reached forward with his right hand, letting the tips of his fingers tug the drawer pull of the top drawer. Inside, a silver semi-auto lay on a fine cloth rag. It was ornately designed with gold inlaid engraving and walnut grips.

Jeff retrieved the piece of art that doubled as a weapon, dropped the clip out and checked that it was loaded. Quickly shoving the clip back in, he clutched the top of the gun's slide with his left hand and pulled it back. Holding it there, Jeff peered through the open ejection port to the tip of bullet ready to make its way from the magazine clip into the barrel. With a sigh, he released the slide, letting it spring forward into position, taking the round inside the firing chamber.

Aiming the loaded and cocked pistol toward the yard, he pointed back and forth from tree to tree before latching his thumb onto the hammer and tugging the trigger, slowly guiding the hammer down into its closed position.

Jeff pressed the call button on his cell and waited. He was now standing in the doorway that led from his office out to the deck.

"Antonio," said Jeff, "our issue with the lady lawyer seems to keep getting worse." He was staring down at the wooden planks. "Yes, she's still alive. I think she's eliminated two of my men. Don't know for sure yet. It's not like I can just run down to the hotel and start asking around."

Jeff walked out onto the deck and began to pace while listening.

He continued, "She called me and told me she killed them. Can you believe she had the nerve? She must wanna die? Yeah, a death wish or something."

He stopped and leaned up against the wall. "Yes, Antonio, I do need you to send some guys up here. This is my hometown and I can't be seen or connected with anything that has blood on it. Remember, this was your deal. Yours. You got me into this shit and now it's at my doorsteps here in Montville."

Jeff kicked at two leaves on the deck. "We need this over with. Its already cost me too much trouble and two good men. We'll talk later."

Slipping the phone inside his pocket, he returned to the office through the door, pulling it shut and being sure to lock it behind him.

chapter thirty-eight

Long Branch, New Jersey. One hour southeast of Montville. I'd heard of this place. Nice, touristy, and pricey. Long Branch was one of those postcard places. It *was* the Jersey Shore after all. The beautiful and perfect tan-colored beach ran north and south as far as I could see. The view was littered with hundreds of beach-goers in my line of sight, many were obvious regulars and the rest were even-more-obvious tourists. Countless more extended up and down the beach, all looking the same and all giving their best to look unique.

My rental car was parked in the parking lot of one of the more elegant of hotels. At least, it appeared that way. The rental was by far the junkiest one in the lot. It fit in not-so-perfectly between a Range Rover and a Porsche. Not so very long ago, I was the woman who wanted this. This kind of life.

That was why the long hours. I always wanted the finer life. I'd tell myself and others that I wanted more for my family, for the girls. But the truth was I wanted it for myself. I wanted my family to be high-society. To drive cars like I had parked next to and come to places like this multiple times a year. Take the selfies and post them on the social media so everyone who knew me could see how great my life was.

But Kaitlyn Cline didn't have to foot the bill for this particular trip.

The counter clerk was a beautiful young lady dressed in a flawless skirt suit. Black skirt, black blazer with a crisp white shirt underneath. A perfectly-tied black bowtie topped it all off.

Thankfully, this bill was going to Elmore. I handed the perfect young woman the credit card and ID. "A room for one," I said. "Two nights."

Being so well-practiced in her professionalism, she immediately eyed the name on the card and said, "Of course, Miss Rilley. Is there anything else I can do for you?"

Pinching my shirt at the shoulder, I pulled the fabric away from my body, leaned my head to it and sniffed it. "Yeah, a laundry. Do you have one that I can use?"

Her professional demeanor broke for a slight second when she winced at my crude action. She answered, "Our hotel does provide a laundry service. I'll have someone come to your room to pick up your clothing in a few minutes."

My eyebrows flicked up unintentionally. I smiled and thanked her as she handed me the key card. *Elmore might fuss about this bill*, I thought.

The room overlooked the beach and the endless ocean of blue. The curtains were wide open when I entered and I left them that way, crashing completely nude on the bed soon after handing off my stinky clothes to the laundry guy. I'd wrapped in a towel for the hand-off.

My backpack sat on the chair with the towel and next to me, on each side of the pure white bedsheet, were my two pacifiers. The things that made me feel safe anywhere, the nine-mil and the thirty-eight.

Maybe it was the long night's rest or maybe it was the clean clothes, but morning brought with it an optimism along with the bright-ass sunlight coming in from those curtains that I'd never pulled shut.

Stepping out onto the large concrete patio of the hotel, I walked to the edge near the sand. Only a handful of people were on the beach at this early hour. I stood there with my eyes closed, letting the ocean breeze whip my hair behind me. In the air, I could literally taste the salt of the seawater. Two large palm trees rustled in the wind.

Dressed in my black cargos and even blacker t-shirt, I didn't quite suit the beach bum profile. Even still, the ocean called to me. Letting myself get drawn to it, I found myself strolling toward the wet sand near where the subtle waves were lapping against the shoreline with a hypnotizing sound. I watched as the white foam caps formed on top of small ripples on the water two hundred yards out, eventually crashing into nothing at my feet.

My thoughts drifted off to my mother. I always liked her name, Allie. The name fit her, I guess. That was coming from the memories of my twelve-year-old self. Her smile was an honest smile. When she smiled, she was happy and it was real. You could feel it from her. I felt it.

Dad adored her so much. He'd flirt with her anywhere. Say how good lookin' she was. At restaurants, he'd say things like, "Hey you pretty thing, wanna go home with me tonight?" Mom'd smile and say, "Of course." I saw a love in them that I rarely ever see these days.

People say that loved ones never leave your heart and I'd agree with that. But they never talk about how much it hurts when the memories flood in.

If I didn't make it back from this unplanned mission, what memories would my girls have of me? I knew the answer to that question. Deep down, I knew the answer, and I didn't like it.

The view of the ocean became blurry as my eyes welled up with tears.

Wiping my cheek with my arm, I turned north and walked along the shore. In an attempt to put the previous thoughts out of my head, I focused on a plan. A plan to put a bullet in Jeff Mitchell's head and get away without being noticed. Part of me wanted to get it done from a distance, anonymously. But another part of me wanted to be able to look him in the eyes. I wanted him to see me, to acknowledge me, and to fear me. I wanted his end to be ... personal.

Time had escaped me and I had wandered north a good distance. People were beginning to drift in and speckle the beach with towels, ice chests, and folding chairs. In my aimless strolling, I'd ended up in front of another hotel with its own patio area and even a swimming pool surrounded by a short black-iron fence. Pairs of lounge chairs were scattered around the pool with little white tables for drinks between each pair.

My attention was caught by one of the two ladies relaxing in the lounge chairs facing the beach. The ladies weren't together, evident by the three empty chairs between them. The lady on the right, though, caught my eye.

She was ...

I'd seen her before.

The blonde ponytail, white shirt and blue jean shorts.

An attractive woman.

The kind of woman a person remembers.

Careful not to make my stare known, I walked into an area of more concentrated new arrivals to the beach. Many were just standing around, some were setting up chairs, while others tried to stab at the sand with their umbrellas. They made no note of me. Taking quick glances in the woman's direction, I felt confident that I'd crossed paths with her before.

The diner.

Yes, she walked in the last time I was there visiting with Shirley.

That was her.

The blonde.

She'd walked in alone.

Coincidence? Couldn't be.

I was being followed.

There was a separation between the hotel and another building where people were coming in from the parking lot. Picking my way south along the beach and keeping myself in among the more crowded areas, I slowly made my way beyond the vision of the hotel pool and nearly even with the alleyway.

In the alley between the two buildings, I stopped and leaned up against a brick wall. Group after group passed in front of me, heading toward the beach, none giving me a second glance.

If she was following me and saw me enter the alley, she'd surely pursue. I waited to see. Minutes went by. Nothing.

Who was she? Someone working for Jeff? The FBI? Who?

If she wasn't going to come to me, I would go to her. I needed to know who she was. If I had to take care of her, I needed to get it done before she relayed anymore information to whoever sent her.

I continued toward the parking lot and the front of the hotel through the alleyway. The tension was growing inside me. It was broad daylight. There were hundreds of eyewitnesses in all directions, cameras on every building, and I was confident there'd be one or two focused in on the swimming pool patio.

Entering through the front lobby door, I was greeted by guy who asked in a very polite manner if I had a room there and if not, why was I coming in. I'm sure they get lots of people just trying to find a restroom or something. That was the way he acted.

"I'm meeting a friend out by the pool," I told him.

He directed me with a smooth wave of his hand. "Straight through those double doors."

I followed his direction and took a fresh towel from a cabinet as I approached the double doors that led out to the pool. Through the glass, I could see her blonde hair. Her back was to me. She was four chairs to the right of the doors and looking out to the ocean. Her feet were crossed in front of her with a loose flipflop dangling off of her toes.

Stopping at the doors, I turned briefly, putting my back to the wall and using that instant to reach back and remove the thirty-eight from its holster. Quickly, I brought it forward and covered it with the folded towel. Palm upright. The pistol held sideways under the towel gave the disguise of anyone simply carrying a towel out to the pool.

In as smooth a movement as any tourist, I pushed through the doors and strolled to the back of her chair. Without hesitation, I leaned over her from behind, placing my left hand on her shoulder and touching her back through the chair's webbing with the muzzle of the thirty-eight. I pressed it into her back firmly so there'd be no mistake in her mind. Placing my mouth next to her ear, I whispered, "Who are you?"

She smelled of nice perfume.

Her gaze never left the ocean. "Hi, Kait," she said in the way someone greets an old friend.

"Who are you?" I repeated.

"I'm Terra," she answered. "We haven't officially met yet. Monica sent me."

Keeping my hand on her shoulder and the thirty-eight in her spine, I asked, "Why? I don't believe you."

She showed no sign of fear or discomfort. "Monica wanted me to be around, but not seen. In case you got into any trouble."

"You've been seen now," I said.

"You are correct, Kait. You're very good," she said, turning her head up to me smiling. "A natural, I might say," she added.

I didn't have anything else to say or ask. I kept my position for a few more awkward seconds.

"Sit down," said Terra, "let's chat. Get to know each other. Your hotel ambush was rather impressive. Quick. Effective. Professional."

Walking around to the lounge chair on her right, I took a seat and reclined back, keeping the towel over my right hand with the thirty-eight held pointed to her from underneath. I still was not fully trusting of her.

The door behind us flung open. My nerves, which were already on end, jumped and my head flung around to see a group of young kids fly through the door wearing swimming trunks and carrying towels.

"Easy now, Kait," Terra joked. "Relax."

I rested my back against the reclined lounge chair again and focused on the beach just as Terra was doing. All the while, keeping aware of her in my peripheral vision. "How'd you know about the hotel?" I asked.

"I saw it. I was watching."

I turned to her. "I don't believe you."

She cracked another smile, keeping her eyes on the horizon. "I watched from the room across."

"How?"

She finally faced me. "Your room was at the end. Mine was across the parking on the other end. I watched with a thermal scope. Any heat source shows up as red and orange images. Let me ask, what did you say to him?"

"Who?"

"The man you stood over before finishing him off. What'd you say? Did you ask any intel? Did he give you any?"

My thoughts shot back to that brief conversation about choices ... and him begging me not to ...

Terra asked again. "Did he give you any info?"

"No," I answered, "he didn't."

"Hmm," she said, sounding unconvinced.

We both let our eyes gravitate toward the ocean waves again and I said, "Look, Terra, or whoever you are, you can go back to wherever you came from. I don't need you following me."

"But Monica —"

I interrupted, "I don't care what Monica wants at this point. Leave me alone."

"As you say, Kait. As you say," she said. "But Monica wanted me to ask you something."

"What?"

"When you complete your current mission, she'd like for you to contact her and Elmore. They want to talk to you."

"About what?" I asked.

"They want to talk to you about work."

"Work?"

"Yeah, a job. You know, work with us."

I could hardly believe my ears. "Who is *us*?"

Terra sat upright and turned toward me in the chair, placing her feet on the warm concrete. "The Organization."

"No," I hissed. "Just no. When this is done, I'm done. I'm going back to my normal life."

Terra stood, grinned at me and said, "See ya, Kait. I'm gonna like working with you." Spinning around, she disappeared through the doors into the hotel.

chapter thirty-nine

The short meeting with Terra left me flustered for the rest of the day and into the night. A job? The Organization? The thought of calling either Dad or Monica to clarify things passed through my mind a few times, but I kept deciding against it. I didn't care. After Jeff, I was done. Done. Out. But I was never really in. Though it seemed Terra and Monica felt otherwise.

Jeff. Ah, Jeff.

I wondered how he was doing. Had he calmed down some? Was he still going crazy trying to find me?

Climbing under the covers for my last night at the Jersey Shore hotel, I tried to clear my mind of him. After all, this would be his last night of sleep above ground. And I hoped he'd get a good rest.

My own sleep wasn't so peaceful. One long dream of Mom filled the night. A dream that haunted me often. A dream of that day at the gas station in Phoenix. The robbery lasted only seconds, but the replay of it seemed to last all night. Over and over again. I saw the large man run inside the building holding the shotgun. He was wearing a mask and he entered shooting. My mom was hit first, followed by an elderly man near one of the aisles. Then lastly, the cashier after he handed over the money. I'll never forget those few seconds. Although he was wearing a black ski mask, I still remembered two details about him after all these years. His long black braided ponytail and the tattoo. I saw it clearly as he ran by the car. It was a tattoo of a black panther. It was climbing up the topside of his right forearm.

I awoke after the sun was already above the horizon, and sitting up, I gathered my two weapons into my lap and simply meditated there. A purposeful silence to help me forget the dream and prepare myself for the day to come.

To buy some time and get a good meal in before sunset, I found myself pulling into the diner again. In my mind, I called it Shirley's Place. The food *was* actually good. I could see her through the large windows as I parked. She was unmistakable as she leaned over a booth, wiping it down.

"Hey, Shirley," I said as I walked inside.

"Lordy, Lordy, look what the cat done dragged in again." She was all smiles. "Come over here, dear, and have a seat. It's been a couple days, we got some catchin' up to do."

I slid into the slick vinyl booth seat. Shirley came to the end of my table and slapped her notepad against her hand. "Let's get an order in for you first. You look starved."

"A plain-ol' burger and fries sounds good."

"Girl, I think that's what you got last time," she said. "You sure you don't wanna try something else?"

I shook my head. "No, I like the burgers. They're good. Really."

"I'll get this order in and be back in a jiffy." She took her notepad and walked away behind the swinging door.

I stared out of the window to the setting sun, wondering what Jeff was up to at that moment.

Shirley pushed back through the door and slipped into the booth across from me. "Alright, spill the beans. Oh, I never did ask your name."

"Sorry," I said, "my name's Sarah."

She stuck out her hand and said, "Well, Sarah, nice to meet you again."

Reaching out, I shook her hand firmly. "You too, Ms. Shirley."

"The boy," she said, leaning forward over the table. "You get that boy figured out? You dump him? Come on, Sarah, I need some gossip. Today's been dull."

She was so youthful for such an aged woman. "He didn't show up last time. So, I didn't get to talk to him. But I'm gonna end it tonight, I think."

"Good girl," Shirley said with a stern expression. Eyes squinted. Mouth squeezed shut. "Get rid of that boy?"

I still don't know why I was so drawn to this woman. In another time, I could have had a serious connection with her. She must surely have a family. I asked, "Ms. Shirley, do you have a Mr.?"

Her head went side to side. "I don't. Had one forty-some-odd years ago, though."

"Oh, I'm sorry. I didn't mean to pry."

"No worries, little lady. It's life." She grinned and looked out to the parking lot. "The one I had was a good one while he was around." Her grin grew to a smile. "We had us some fun in those early years. He was a handsome one. Tall too. Dark hair. Every girl's dream. We had our son and times got tough. He couldn't take it and he run off."

I repeated the generic response, "I'm sorry."

"It's ok. It was a long time ago. I started workin' as a waitress and raised up my boy right here in this town." Her face lit up. "We survived. My boy and I."

"Is he still around? I mean, do you get to see him much?"

"Oh, yes," she said. "He grew up into a successful businessman and lives a few miles away. He's rich now. Got a good life."

I sat back in the booth, happy to hear a good end to her story. "That's nice, Ms. Shirley."

"You might wonder why I work here if my boy is so successful. I'll tell you. I told him I don't want him to have to take care of me. I'm good with my paycheck. Got a nice little house on the edge of town. Don't need nothin' more. He does keep me in a good car, though. He says he doesn't want me stranded somewhere in a broke-down vehicle. So every two years, he gets me a new car. Not a fancy one or anything, just a basic one to get me around town safely."

"You must be very proud of him," I said.

"I am. I am." She got up and straightened her apron. "I'll go get your food so you don't starve to death."

chapter forty

About an hour after sunset, I slowly drove past Jeff's front gate. It was closed, just as before, with nothing new to see. On the brick column that held the mailbox, a single light mounted at the top cast a circle of light down onto the driveway.

Passing up the drive, I took a right onto the next street and pulled to a stop on the side of the road in front of another estate's iron fencing. It was dark but not completely black. The stars were out as was a sliver of the moon.

Pulling my backpack to me from the passenger seat, I opened it and made sure the nine millimeter was in good order. I popped the clip out and then shoved it in again, drew back the slide, watching a fresh cartridge get drawn into the firing chamber and finally, I unscrewed the silencer. After setting the backpack on the floorboard, I worked the silencer into the left cargo pocket of my pants and the pistol itself, into the right cargo pocket. Reassembly would take place on location.

Next, I moved the thirty-eight to the front hip pocket and reached down in the dark to the lower part of the car's dash, feeling around. Finding the hood lever, I tugged it.

I'd learned long ago that no one bothers a car with its hood up. Even the police. But without appearing in distress, a car parked somewhere it shouldn't be parked tends to raise suspicion and curiosity. A car with a hood up, though … everyone ignores it.

The image of Jeff Mitchell was cemented into my head. I didn't need to see the picture Monica sent me again but it'd be best. Powering up my phone, I clicked on Monica's last message and glared into Jeff's eyes. He was a handsome man, easy to pick out from a crowd. And if I can get the chance, I'd like to see into those eyes in person.

I put the phone on silent, shut it down, and retrieved the driving gloves from the console. Slipping them on slowly, I intertwined my fingers together, securing the fit.

Stepping out, I went to the front of the car raising the hood all the way open. Intuitively, I took in a deep breath as if my body expected it to calm my nerves. It didn't.

On my walk to the front gate, all was quiet. No people, no cars, nothing. It's said that money can't buy happiness. I don't know if that's true or not, but this neighborhood is evidence that money *can* buy one thing. And that is privacy.

Nearing the gate, my pace dropped to a slow stroll. There could be a camera at the gate and I couldn't take that chance. The iron fencing near the sidewalk was made up of square metal bars spaced a few inches apart and standing six feet tall. Every twenty feet, there was a large brick column like the one at the driveway with the mailbox. The fencing was bolted to those columns, creating what was honestly a really nice and expensive fence.

I halted and listened for any approaching cars. None. Jamming my foot against the brick column and using tight handholds on the metal bars, I worked my way up onto the top, then over, letting myself fall as silently as possible into the grass and leaves on the other side. Standing quickly, I rested up against the column panting. I nervously felt my pockets to make sure none of the weaponry had fallen out from my drop.

All was good.

Through the trees, lights could be seen and I cautiously worked toward them step by step. The dry leaves on the ground made my trek much noisier than I'd have liked. Noise was bad. Always. Not only could it give away a location, it prevented the hearing of other important sounds in the distance, such as a car starting or a house door shutting.

After covering more ground, I'd made it halfway to the mansion. The trees were thinning and I could see the outline of the driveway to my right about a hundred feet away. The silhouette of the house and part of a huge deck becoming visible. Some lights beaming down onto the deck gave off a light blue glow.

I kept moving forward. To the target.

My breathing became more shallow with each step.

The thin forest of trees had opened up. Shadows of the tree trunks that had served as my cover would end in a few more feet. Beyond that was the beginning of the large manicured grass yard. Scanning my options, one more batch of trees existed. They were on the other side of the driveway. A hundred yard distance away. If I made it there, though, it appeared that I would be nearly within pistol range of the deck.

Maybe that would work.

It'd have to.

Taking a moment to study the house which was now in clear view, I was awed by its size. Three stories tall with huge windows covering each level of the right side. Directly in the front, was a four-car garage with garage doors that looked like enormous panels of frosted glass. Very modern. Wrapping around the side of the home on the second level was the deck. Even in the dark with the home lit by the night sky and the many security lights surrounding, it was a sight to behold. I muttered, "This is beyond being rich." The homes I'd seen earlier in the week on my initial drive-by didn't compare to this one.

Returning my focus to the job at hand, I decided that a sprint across into the next group of trees was my singular option. Upon feeling somewhat confident that I'd not be seen, I made the dash across the asphalt drive to the base of the first tree. I pressed in close to the tree, peering around it toward the mansion.

A loud click sounded in the distance behind me. Then the sound of metal wheels or rollers. Two beams of light appeared to bounce off of the trees I'd just come through. Someone had entered the gate. I squatted and worked myself around to the backside of the tree trunk and watched as a long sedan snaked toward me, following the curved driveway. As the headlight beams swept across my tree, I squeezed in tight, directly behind the trunk, watching the light rays illuminate the grass before going black as if the rays themselves had hit an impenetrable wall, then reappearing on the other side.

I sidestepped into the direction of the home until coming to another tree. One of the garage doors opened and the sedan pulled inside.

When the brake lights brightened, the garage door began to drop. Both the driver's and passenger doors swung open as the garage door was midway down and all I was able to see were the blue jeans and leather boots of whoever stepped out of the passenger side. That was it.

The garage door had closed, leaving only their blurred silhouettes visible through the frosted glass.

It was him.

It was Jeff.

I hadn't seen his face, but I had a hunch, a strong hunch.

Hurriedly, I bounded from tree to tree like a child, gaining ground and getting nearer to the home. Closer to the deck with all the large windows. As I moved, I kept my eyes on the mansion. Twice I saw movement inside. Both times were only brief flashes, giving me no indication of how many people were inside. Nor any clue of a common gathering place or room. If I'd been more experienced at this type of thing, I'd have surely planned this better.

Ahead, I could see three tree trunks together in a tight grouping. Two of them growing from the same base that created a fork low to the ground. They were the closest to the mansion, being maybe a hundred-fifty feet from the edge of the porch. Reaching the forked set, I settled into a squat with my back against one of the large trunks.

Even though I was in close proximity to the home, I was well hidden. Between my trees and the mansion were large bright circles of light thrown onto the ground from the various security lights mounted on the walls of the house. The deck possessed an array of small decorative lanterns that cast a steady glow onto its surface. None of the lighting reached my small tree grove.

I was invisible.

Pulling the nine millimeter out of one cargo pocket, I also retrieved the silencer from the other. Methodically screwing them together as if it were meditation. Meditation as a means of preparing myself.

I turned around, rested on my knees facing Jeff's mansion, and watched patiently from behind the safety of my trees.

It was only a matter of minutes before I realized there were at least three men and one woman in the building. Living in a home with so many large glass windows must be amazing during the day, but after the sun goes down, the windows become wide-open portals giving anyone near a view into the private life of those within. Some of the windows had shades, but the silhouettes still were still very visible against the backlight of the room.

On the second floor, a man entered the far right room. He shut the door behind him. His back was to me. He was tall with dark hair wearing a red polo shirt, jeans, and ... boots. Pacing nervously in front of a big desk, he had both hands clasped behind his neck. The details of his face blocked by his elbows.

One room and three windows over on the same second floor, two more men sat on a couch watching TV. And the shape that I'd figured to be female had gone upstairs to the third level and flipped on a light. Her form disappeared as her destination led her away from the window and out of my sight.

The realization hit me. There were simply too many ears floating around for me to get inside for any private time with Jeff, which I so desired. It would be too risky.

With his repetitive back and forth walking in the room, I could technically make the shot from where I was. If I were positive that was him and he wasn't behind that damn glass. If he were in the open, I could take him easily. But the glass between us. Damned the glass. The angle of impact was the issue. I wasn't in a direct line with him, perpendicular to the glass pane. Ideally, if I were, the bullet's trajectory could remain mostly intact, only loosing velocity. But from down here at this angle, I worried that any deflection from the bullet passing through the glass would result in a miss. With a vital loss of surprise.

His pacing stopped near one of the large glass panes at the furthest point of the room. He reached out, twisting a lever. A door. Jeff tugged it open. It swung in toward the room and he stepped into the open cavity of the doorway. He rested his body up against the door frame with his arms crossed out of what seemed to be a mood of disgust.

It was him.

No mistake.

He was in full view of the lighting from the deck.

His eyes.

It may have been my brain playing tricks on me, but I could see into his eyes. He was staring off into the black distance, but I felt that I could see his soul.

Perfect.

Hold that pose, Jeff, I thought.

With both hands tight, I raised the nine-mil between the fork of the tree trunks, using the rightmost one to rest the outside of my forearm against.

My thumb tugged the hammer back until the *click*.

Steady.

Steady.

Lightly, I guided my index finger onto the trigger, applying only enough pressure to feel the tension.

Steady.

In one quick motion, Jeff pulled away from the door frame, walking back inside the room.

Shit.

"Patience, Kait," I whispered to myself. I kept the pistol cocked, relaxing only slightly.

Inside, Jeff began pacing again. Removing his cell phone from the pocket of his blue jeans, he held it at his side as he paced, flipping the screen toward him every few seconds. He was waiting. For a call or a text. But he was waiting and he wasn't nearly as patient as I.

I'd sit here as long as I needed to. I'd be patient. I'd wait for what'd be the final moment of these previous weeks of hell.

I'd wait.

In a sick way, I'd wait because I wanted to be sure that I got some bit of pleasure from it.

The perfect shot.

The perfect kill.

The perfect revenge.

I'd wait.

The adrenalin pulsed through me. It blurred the fact that what I was doing was essentially wrong. It blurred the lawyer brain in me. It only allowed for the clear vision of the ... hunt.

I'd been the prey ever since my plane landed in Colorado. Now the tables have turned.

Jeff approached the door again, stalling just shy of the opening. Looking at his phone one last time, he shoved it back into his pocket and crossed his arms. The shallow ripple of his forearm muscles flinched and his biceps bulged some, stretching the sleeve of his polo shirt.

I tensed.

My grip on the nine-mil tightened.

I took one big deep breathe in hopes to slow my heart rate.

Yes.

With his arms still crossed, Jeff strolled out onto the wooden deck and walked to the railing, stopped and spread his feet apart in an over-masculine stance. The stance of a leader.

Bracing my arm against the tree truck again, I sighted down the barrel, aligning the front and rear sight together and aiming them just above and in front of Jeff Mitchell's ear. My index finger coming to rest against the trigger's tension again. I inhaled once, held my breath and ...

Two beams of lights coming up fast from the left of me startled Jeff and myself. Both of us turned our heads to see a white SUV barreling up the driveway and coming to a quick stop in front of the garage doors.

Four men climbed out of the SUV, the passenger being the most visual of group. An old man with silver hair, wearing a light-colored full suit. In the darkened atmosphere, I couldn't tell if it were white or light tan. It didn't matter, the guy was put together.

The driver was a younger lad dressed in tan slacks and a dark blue button-up short-sleeved shirt made of a shiny fabric. It glittered in the lights. He and the old man went briskly to a set of stairs leading up to the deck where Jeff was watching them.

The other two who were in the back seat took their time getting out. They trailed behind, dressed much less impressive. Younger and lacking importance, judging from appearance. They followed up the stairs. Something about them felt all too familiar, though.

I kept my eyes on them, ignoring the old man and the driver. Once the last two guys stepped onto the deck in better light, I nearly lost my breath. I sat back from my kneeling position, letting my butt rest on the heels of my shoes. I knew those two.

I could almost feel the healed bullet wounds in my back begin to burn. Those two. They were the two who ran me off of the road in Aspen and shot me, leaving me for dead.

My mind flashed with the memory of when I looked up from the crumpled car to the one with the slicked-back dark hair. I remember seeing him point the pistol down the mountain to me and firing. I remember hearing the other guy fussing. I remember his last words of "I got her" as they echoed in my head.

My emotions were getting the best of me. I wanted to kill every single one of them standing on that deck. I wanted to see blood coming from each of them.

I could do it. Five on the deck and two inside.

I could do it.

"Calm down, girl," I whispered to myself as if Dad were standing over my shoulder. Turning this into a wild-west shootout would do nothing but get me killed.

Jeff extended his hand to the old man in the suit, but the old man pushed Jeff's hand aside and reached both arms around Jeff, pulling him into a hug. Jeff hugged him back with a visual discomfort. The old man released his embrace and patted Jeff's arms with his hands. No words had been spoken from either.

The two men of Jeff's who'd been sitting on the couch inside stepped out, expressionless. They both eyed the old man's entourage.

Maybe they'd all shoot each other and I wouldn't have to do a damn thing. That would be the easy way out. I watched with anticipation, wishing for the tension in the air to dissipate. I still needed my revenge. I'd only be satisfied with any deaths being dealt from my own bullets.

The old man turned his back to Jeff and looked out over the dark yard. In a heavy accent, he said, "Señor Jeff, you have a fantastic home. I now see why you like it here." He reached into the inside pocket of his suit coat and removed a cigar. "I offer you one of these again. Do you wish?" he asked, showing it to Jeff.

Jeff shook his head. "No."

"Ah, that is right, you like your — what are they? Marlboros? Si, like the cowboy on TV?"

"Yes, Antonio. Like the cowboy on TV."

Antonio pulled a cigar cutter and a Zippo lighter from his other coat pocket, snipped the end off of the cigar and lit it, sucking in deep to get it fired up. "Señor Jeff, please smoke with me," he said to Jeff. "Get one of your Marlboro cigarettes and share this moment with me. Please." Antonio made a motion with his hand to Jeff as a call to action.

Jeff's two men had eased up some, but remained behind Jeff by a few feet. Antonio's men stayed closer to the stairs and had temporarily lost interest in the meeting. They were scoping out the house and grounds.

Without taking his eyes off of Antonio, Jeff fiddled with the small pocket of his polo shirt, retrieving a pack of cigarettes. I recognized the famous red and white packaging. Flipping the lid and taking one out, he set in his mouth.

Antonio thumbed the Zippo and offered it Jeff with the flame bouncing above the bright silver casing.

Jeff returned the lighter, took a long drag on the Marlboro and both men stood side by side staring out over the estate. Twice their gaze passed right over my location where I still sat on my heels pondering what to do.

After some silence, Jeff was the first to speak. "Antonio, I don't have the time for useless formalities. I need to have our issue taken care of. And the sooner, the better."

"Of course, Señor Jeff, that is why I came. I will leave two of my men here to work with yours on this ... issue." Antonio paused, then began again with a slower and almost monotone voice, "Señor Jeff, I do understand your urgency, but we still have time on our side. The trial has not yet begun."

Jeff's temper flared. "Look, Antonio, like I said on the phone, you got me into this. You were supposed to have that lawyer bitch taken care of. I provided the location, and your men were to get it done. None of this shit was my idea. And now she's over here in my hometown, calling me on the fucking phone!"

My jaw dropped open and I let my arms fall into my lap, still holding the nine-mil. It was him all along. The old man. The old man ordered my hit and Jeff tried to finish it. It was both of them. But who was this Antonio guy?

Antonio said to Jeff, "With my men's help, this minor inconvenience will be handled, Señor Jeff. I assure you. And once this is done, we may resume our talks of territory distribution."

"Fine, I'll leave town for a week," said Jeff. "I can't be anywhere around here with this going in my own town."

Antonio smiled. "Yes, you go take some time to yourself. Have fun. Meet some señoritas. I'll go back to Florida and return after this has been resolved."

Jeff turned to Antonio and leaned in close. I hoped that I'd still be able to hear. Instinctively, I leaned forward between the two tree trunks. He told Antonio, "I've told you once and I'll tell you again, if I even get a feeling that this is going bad or that you are turning on me, I'll make sure that I kill you myself." Jeff took a step back. "Remember that. Always remember that." Jeff glared at Antonio's men who had been watching and listening intently, sensing the tension between the two.

Antonio put out his cigar on the deck railing and tossed the remainder out into the grass. He spun to walk away, but put his right hand onto Jeff's shoulder. "Señor Jeff, there is no need for this harsh talk. We are colleagues, you and I. Competitors maybe, but still colleagues." Antonio walked toward the steps. "Have a good vacation, Señor Jeff. We will talk soon."

Jeff simply nodded without a word.

Passing by his men, Antonio flipped his finger to the guy with slicked-back dark hair, "Let us go now. Come drive."

"Yes sir, Mr. Fuentes," he said as they both exited down the steps, leaving the other two men awkwardly still standing on the porch with Jeff and his men.

My mind spun with this new information. I have another target, Antonio Fuentes.

Jeff watched the SUV drive off and went toward the office door. He stopped before entering and told the group of four men, "You guys get to know each other. I'm going to pack." He flicked his half burnt cigarette over the deck into the yard.

The rental car was just as I'd left it with its hood up when I made my way back to it. I felt an emptiness inside because Jeff Mitchell would get to sleep another night or two. If only he knew how lucky he was for that luxury. I myself needed a good night of sleep as well.

On the way to the hotel room, I asked myself, "Kait, is it possible to kill two birds with one stone? Is there a way?" I was too beat to come up with an answer.

chapter forty-one

The knock at the front door startled Daniel. It was late in the evening and he'd just sent the girls to bed. Opening the door, he let out a loud and disappointed sigh upon seeing Scott Bertrand standing under the porch light in what appeared to be his same boring suit.

The thought of simply shutting the door passed through Daniel's mind and Scott knew it. Scott put out his hand, stepping into the doorway and passively forcing his way into another conversation.

"Mr. Cline," said Scott, "I need to talk."

Reaching up and straightening his glasses with his eyes closed, Daniel huffed, "Ok, I guess." He motioned for the agent to enter with a quick flip of his head. "Not too long, though."

Scott entered only a few feet and stood facing Daniel. "Thanks, I'll only be a minute or two."

"Wanna sit?" asked Daniel.

"No," answered Scott. "Mr. Cline, I've been doing more research into your wife's past."

"Yeah."

"You had told me last time that she didn't have any hobbies or anything when you met. Is that correct?"

"Yes, it is. Why?"

Scott pushed the flaps of his sport coat aside and stuffed his hands into the pockets of his suit pants. "Mr. Cline, were you not aware of her expertise with firearms?"

"She said she used to shoot in tournaments. She had some old trophies, but I figured it was nothing. You know, just amateur stuff."

Scott nodded and looked down at his feet. "Also, her dad. You said he currently resides in New Mexico?"

"I did."

"His name is Chris Falcon?"

Daniel pursed his lips at the line of odd questions. "Yes, it is."

Scott's eyes met Daniel's. "I can find no record of him existing after the explosion. All information shows him as deceased. Says he died in the home explosion in Phoenix. Do you know his address, Mr. Cline?"

Daniel's face softened as he tried to jog his memory but realizing that nothing was there. "As a matter of fact, I don't know his address."

"Can you remember how to get to his house?"

"I've only been there once and Kaitlyn was driving. It was late at night and I really wasn't paying any attention to directions." Daniel's eyes went to the ceiling as his brain attempted to dig more details out of thin air.

Scott immediately asked, "What was the nearest large city? Do you know that?"

"Yeah, Farmington. I remember that."

"What direction did you drive from Farmington?"

"Agent Scott, I don't know," Daniel replied. "I was tired and Kaitlyn was driving. I have no idea."

Scott pulled his hands out of his pockets, dangling a car key in his right one. "I'll take off now. Thanks, Mr. Cline."

"Sorry I'm not much help."

Walking toward the door, Scott twisted the doorknob, then stopped and turned to Daniel. "Mr. Cline, has your wife tried to contact you?"

"No!" said Daniel loudly. "She hasn't. I have not heard her voice since that last message. This is sending me up the wall and all I want is to have her back. Every time you come here and ask questions, you seem to insinuate something different each time. Just find my wife … please."

Scott opened the door saying, "We're doing what we can."

Watching Scott pull the door closed on his way out, Daniel mumbled, "Yeah, right."

chapter forty-two

Another night, another generic hotel room. So many days and nights have become scrambled in my mind. Every hotel is different in a way and every one is the same.

"Here's your key, Miss Rilley," the counter clerk said, handing me the key and my receipt. "You're in room 310. The elevator is down that hall or the stairs are right there." She pointed to a set of iron stair treads covered in raggedy victorian-patterned carpet that was begging to come apart where it saw the most foot traffic.

I chose the stairs.

As soon as I entered the room and latched the door behind me, I tossed my backpack on the bed and fished my phone out of my pocket. Thumbing to the search engine on the phone, I typed *Antonio Fuentes* into the keyboard.

Lots of hits popped up. *Florida. Businessman. Importer of Cuban goods.* I sat down on the bed and began to click into and read some of the links. They were mostly old local news articles with headlines such as: *Philanthropist* and *Champion for local Cubans' rights in Southern Florida*.

"Hmm, a freakin' saint to the people it appears," I said to myself. "I guess I'll help push him into full-blown martyr status."

Setting the phone on the bed next to me, I let myself fall back flat onto the comforter. I spoke to the ceiling as if it could talk back, "Dang, I have to go to Florida. Florida. I guess it makes sense though now. Matteo Bianchi has his head on the chopping block for his empire of drug trade in the central East Coast and these two see an opportunity." The light's reflection onto the ceiling flickered as if it understood me. "Antonio's running the drugs on the Southern Seaboard while Jeff's in charge of the northern. Genius actually. If they can get Matteo to go under, then they can split up his territory." I squinted one eye to my invisible friend, the ceiling. "Dang good business sense, though. Sure is. All they have to do is kill a prosecuting attorney for Matteo's nephew's trial. So simple, right?"

I slipped my hand under my back and pulled the thirty-eight out, aiming it at the ceiling and focusing the sights on the tiniest of shadows cast up from the lamp next to me. Lying there on my back with both hands steadying my tiny little companion, I slowed my breathing and let my muscles relax, keeping the sights motionless as long as I could.

I awoke with the phrase stuck in my head, *two birds with one stone.*

After a long, hot shower and a really cruddy continental breakfast that consisted of powered eggs with a fake apple juice concentrate, I dialed Monica's number. I really didn't want to call her again but I needed to. It'd be the easiest way to get Antonio's address. But meeting Terra and knowing that she was sent by Monica to follow me still bugged me deeply.

"Good morning, Kait," Monica answered almost too cheerfully.

"Hi, Monica, I need another favor."

"Anything for you, Kait," was her response. "What can I do?"

"An address," I said, "I need another address."

"For whom?" Monica asked.

"Antonio Fuentes. In Florida."

Monica snickered on her end of the line and said, "Gee, Kait, you are quite the traveler as of lately. I'll get on it. Anything else?"

"Yes. I met your friend."

"Who's that?"

"Terra," I said. "She said you sent her."

Monica's voice didn't waver. She sounded neither upset nor surprised when she replied to the statement. "I did send her. I sent her for your protection, and also ours. I need to keep you safe as well as insure the anonymity of our Organization. You are new, Kait. I hope you understand."

"You say *new* like I'm a part of something," I said. "I'm not part of it. Once I'm done with this, I'm done. I won't bug you or Elmore ever again."

Monica spoke as if she never even heard what I'd just told her. "Terra said that you were very impressive in your work. She liked you. Said you were a natural."

"Did you hear me say that I was done?"

"I did."

"And?"

"We shall talk later."

"No, Monica, we won't." I was getting pissed, but I did my best to keep it at bay because I needed one more final address from her.

"Very well," she said. "I'll text you the address when I find it. Go ahead and start driving south."

"Ok, thanks."

Picking up my backpack from off of the hotel bed, I shouldered it and exited the room. I'd do just as she said, start driving south. But I had one other address to swing by first on my trek to Florida, 410 Bowmer Lane in Charlotte.

chapter forty-three

After nine hours of drive time and quite a few lengthy breaks, I entered the city limits of Charlotte shortly after 8:30pm. Deep down, I knew I shouldn't have been there. Dad warned me not contact Daniel or the girls in any way until my mission was done.

However, I now had much more information than at the start of all this. I knew that Jeff's men along with Antonio's were searching for me in New Jersey where I was last known to be. Where I'd left two bodies to show for it. Antonio was on his way back to Florida, if not already there. And Jeff, Jeff had taken time away from everything with his own little vacation to get out of town, who knows where.

Making the last turn onto Bowmer Lane, I slowed, paying attention to every flicker of light and every car. I recognized each one in the numerous driveways. None of them stood out as odd.

Approaching our home, I could see that Daniel's car was gone. The house was dark. Dark inside and dark outside. Not even the front porch light was on. Daniel and girls had not been there recently.

Ours was a nice neighborhood. It'd a been better if the homes were on bigger lots, but it was still ok. Each of the nineteen-fifties homes had its own fenced-in backyard with a small sample of a front, adorned with lush green grass. Contrasting the green yards were the driveways that served each home and the narrow concrete paths leading to the front doors. Looking down the street, there was a continuity in lot design and our few streets seemed to be an early, mid-century version of the cookie-cutter housing that has become so common these days.

Each different in paint color, but similar in design, the homes themselves possessed high-pitch rooflines that made them appear larger than they were. I always felt that the inset front porches were an eye-pleasing design element that added a Victorian appeal.

Only two blocks over from our little section of history was the modern world in all its glory and conveniences. A grocery, a coffee shop, two gas stations, and a liquor store. New America had grown up around old America.

The street was empty and I saw no activity near any of the homes. People were in for the evening. Except my crew, they were most likely having dinner at Daniel's mother's house. They'd be out until even later. Talking was a gift of his mother's. She truly adored Olivia and Mattie. And Daniel, too. She only tolerated me.

I passed our home, noticing how the streetlamp illuminated only what was within its range, leaving the rest of the home to lie in dark shadows.

Two houses past ours was a side street to the right that led to the gas station. I took it, drove the extra block and parked in the back of the station.

No, don't even think about it, my mind said quietly.

Don't do it, Kait.

I turned the engine off and sat there looking through the windshield into the blackness of the alley behind the station.

One clue.

If I left one simple clue, then Daniel would know. He'd know that I wasn't dead. One clue would give him hope. Hope that I was going to come home.

Maybe. That is if he hadn't given up already.

Leaving my backpack in the car, I got out and walked into the station. I had no worry of being recognized by any workers. I'd only been inside once. On that day, nearly four years ago, I noticed it was dirty and it turned me off. Too dirty for an up-and-coming attorney with a second-hand Mercedes.

My how the tables have turned. I'd been wearing these same clothes since San Diego and only washed them once. The very gothic nature of my current appearance was enough to make any late-shift worker weary of me.

Topping it all off was my bad chop-job of a haircut with its sink-dyed black color.

A young man wearing a flannel shirt with the typical patchy beard of a juvenile sat on a stool behind the counter, playing on his phone.

"May I have a scrap of paper and a pen, please?" I asked, standing in the small opening between the acrylic cases of scratch-off tickets.

He never answered. He only leaned forward without moving from his stool, tossing a pen onto the counter and pointing to a small notepad behind the acrylic case to my left.

"Thanks," I mumbled, reaching behind the case for the pad. Opening it, I tore out a piece of paper and clicked the pen. I glanced up at the young man only to see that he'd already returned his attention to his phone and way paying me no mind.

I quickly scribbled two words onto my scrap of paper. *I'm alive.*

Leaving the car in the back of the station, I began my short walk. The last thing I needed was to be seen parking a car in front of the house. In the dark of night, our charming neighborhood was much less inviting. There was something about shadows and the empty blackness where the beams from the street lamps failed to reach.

In that blackness lived what people were most afraid of ... the unknown.

I tipped my head down, allowing the hair to fall forward onto my face, creating somewhat of an identity screen while I made my way from the station and onto Bowmer Lane.

Without skipping a beat, I turned the sharp left onto our personal concrete path that led to the front of our house. I knew no one was inside, but to provide a visually normal action for any onlookers, I rapped at the wooden door with my knuckles once then folded the note and shoved it into the crack between the door and the rubber seal on the doorjamb. Keeping my head down, I briskly returned to my car.

I heard no sounds and I saw no one.

chapter forty-four

Agent Scott Bertrand sat on the sofa facing the front window of the small vacant house on Bowmer Lane that the FBI rented for surveillance. It was the closest home available within eyesight of Daniel and Kaitlyn's place, six houses down. Much further than he'd have liked.

He'd been staked out there since the day after his first meeting with Daniel. There was something about Kaitlyn's disappearance that didn't add up. Over the weeks and countless hours watching the Cline house through the blinds with his binoculars, he'd worn down an area on the fabric of a sofa from his constantly sitting in the same spot. The sofa was freebee, came with house. It was positioned diagonally across the mostly empty living room. From where he had set it, Scott could sit on the sofa comfortably with a view through the window toward the Cline's. With the blinds lowered, but twisted open, his daily surveillance went unnoticed to any outside eyes.

The living room was always dark. At night, though, it was a dreadful black. No lights were turned on aside from the bathroom one which was completely out of the street's view.

Scott flipped his wrist to see the time. Knowing his replacement would be there soon didn't make the last few minutes any easier. The TV shows did a good job of romanticizing the life of an FBI agent with all the action and shooting, but they leave out the fact that ninety-nine point nine percent of the job was often deathly boring. This job revolved around waiting and more waiting. Hours upon hours of lonely time spent only with his own thoughts.

Scott had a gut-feeling and he was rarely wrong.

Patience being one of his best virtues as an agent.

He'd wait. He'd wait however long it took.

Everyone slips up, even the best of criminals. And the only way to be there and see a slip-up is to … wait.

Under the streetlight at the corner past the Cline's home, Scott noticed a figure turn the corner on foot. In other neighborhoods, that wouldn't seem odd, but he'd spent enough time studying Bowmer Lane and its residents to know that rarely did anyone walk around their homes after dark. It wasn't a street of night owls and party animals. Just the opposite.

He bent forward and raised the binoculars to his eyes, turning the focus knob with his index finger until the moving shadow came in to focus.

A female.

Unrecognizable.

Moving rather quickly and the most interesting fact to him was that she knew where she was going. She was all-too familiar with her route. Her head was down, but she was set on her destination.

Scott scooted to the edge of the sofa and said aloud, "Ah, Kaitlyn, is that you?"

The figure reached the Cline home, then spun toward it, walking on the pathway up to the door. Scott saw the knock and the speedy slip of something in the door.

He stood up with the binoculars still at his face and stepped closer to the blinds as if the movement would enlarge his view even more. "You little devil, you," he said, watching the figure retrace the route from where she came.

As soon as Kaitlyn's shape disappeared, making her right turn onto the intersecting street, Scott dropped the binoculars on the sofa and went to the door, unlocking it and walking out. He crossed the street and headed directly to the Cline home as if in a trance. Kaitlyn left something and he needed to see what it was.

He grinned.

Validation.

Validation that his hunches were correct.

Once reaching the home, Scott skipped the concrete path, opting to go straight through the grass.

There it was. Poking out of the crack in the door, a small corner of paper was showing just above the deadbolt lock. It was crumpled from Kaitlyn's attempt to push it in. Tugging at it carefully so not to tear it, Scott pulled it out and opened it. Twisting around and holding the paper toward the street lamp, he read the two simple words written. Folding the paper back up, he stuffed it into the inside pocket of his sports coat.

Knowing he couldn't be seen standing around in front of the home, he hurriedly scampered down the block and crossed the street.

A set of headlights rounded the corner just as he set foot inside dark living room. Shutting the door behind him, Scott watched the headlights pass his window and turn into the Cline's driveway.

chapter forty-five

Roughly eight more hours of driving. I'd hoped I would've been done by now. I shouldn't be sneaking around slipping notes inside the door of my own home. I should be sitting on the couch with the girls, telling them how much I loved them and how much I missed them. I should be telling Daniel that things were going to be different from here on. I should be beginning my new life, the life I've dreamed of so often since that day in Aspen. *I shouldn't be driving to damned Florida.*

Jacksonville, Florida at two in the morning was nothing special. At 2am, there is nowhere that looks very special. Maybe Vegas. Vegas never shuts down.

Pulling off of the interstate into the parking lot of a truck stop, my body was tired. I was tired. Finding a parking spot in the back corner away from the security lights, I backed in and reclined my seat. I don't even remember closing my eyes.

The phone ringing sounded like a distant dream. I shifted around in the seat, still mostly asleep. And uncomfortable. The phone rang again. My eyes popped open and I reached for it. Through blurry vision, I made out Monica's name as I rubbed my eyes. I tapped the icon to answer.

"Hello," I said, noticing that it was still very early.

Monica chirped, "Hi there, I have some intel for you."

Realizing that it was even earlier where she was in California, I told her, "Monica, you didn't have to call me this early. You should still be asleep."

"I know. It's fine," she said. "I was up early anyway and I knew that you could use these addresses."

"Ok. But as usual, I don't have anything to write with. Tell them to me, then text them." I was lying flat on my back in the reclined driver's seat, staring up at the stained headliner.

"The first one is a commercial address. It might be a warehouse or some type of storage. And the other must be a home. Mr. Fuentes is like a local hero down there. He was easy to find. Almost too easy. And I didn't see anything that had a bad smell to it, Kait."

"Yeah?" I said under my breath, listening to her.

"Kait, are sure he is your guy?" asked Monica. "He just seems too clean. Are you sure?"

"I'm sure, Monica. I'm very sure," I answered. "I'll

know if there's a mistake when I see him. I did get a good visual."

"Ok," she said in a long, drawn-out tone of slight disbelief. "I trust you. Just make sure. And Kait…"

"Yes?"

"Do you need me to send someone? I have a team-member within a few hours of you."

"No, Monica. But thanks anyway. Tell me the addresses please."

"Here you go. The commercial building is located at 4356 5th Street in the city of DeLand. The address that I feel would be his home or residence is at 739 Ocean Shore Boulevard in Daytona Beach. I'll send them in a text after we hang up like you asked."

"Thanks. Oh, Monica," I said, "if this works out like I expect … you won't hear from me ever again."

"Now, Kait," she said in her ever-so-sweet voice. "You just be careful. Be efficient. Be invisible. And if you reconsider our offer, call me."

I didn't reply. Taking the phone away from my ear, my thumb hit disconnect and I waited for the text.

I set the phone down on the center console, rubbed my scalp with the palms of my hands and reached down to the lever, returning the seat to its upright position.

The sun had just broken the horizon and some of the truckers were moving about in the truck parking a few hundred feet away. Four stood next to their trucks enjoying an early morning smoke, a couple were sipping from mugs, and one was walking toward the building carrying a small bag, likely for toothbrushes and stuff.

Cranking the car's engine, I yawned, put the transmission into drive, and aimed the car south again toward the entrance ramp.

Monica's text dinged in just as I merged into traffic.

I could now imagine my dad doing something like this. This as a job. As he said it, *taking care of business sometimes.* I'd come to see an entirely new side of him recently.

But Mom? I couldn't see it. I couldn't believe it. I could ask Elmore and I'm sure he'd tell me the truth. A part of me would love to know. I shook my head side to side as the bumps from the interstate created a rhythm of *thump, thumps* under the car.

No, I didn't want to know. Even if it was the truth, I didn't want to know. I didn't want to contaminate the memories that I've had of her all these years. I didn't want my brain to try to fill in any missing details. Details like all the times she said she was visiting family out of state. Details like telling me the bruises on her body were from a fall while hiking in the mountains.

No, I didn't need to know. I often close my eyes at times and just remember her smile, her soft voice, and the way she'd say my name.

As the years have gone by, my memories have gotten more choppy and segmented. I can't see or remember entire scenes anymore, my mind tends to focus on the small events. Like watching her stand in front of the mirror brushing her long brown hair. I'd stand in the doorway of the bathroom and watch. Her hair flowed as the brush passed through it. She'd gracefully follow the brush with her fingers, letting the ends of her hair fall from them like fine strands of silk.

Was it really like that? I doubt it. I was only remembering through the eyes of an overly-romantic child who was in awe of the woman she wanted to grow up to be like.

No, I didn't need to know the truth from Elmore.

Daytona Beach was sight to behold, especially on an amazing summer day. I'd turned onto Ocean Shore Boulevard a few miles ahead of my final destination to see the sights. Ocean Shore is a two-lane highway running north and south up the eastern side of Florida near Daytona Beach. It was a beautiful drive, it really was. For those first few miles, there were no buildings at all on my left, leaving a wide open view of the ocean waves rolling onto the shore. The white-caps landed slowly against the sand, almost peacefully, and the green color of the nearby water transformed into an amazing deep blue further out.

It was a perfect drive that would have only been more perfect if I'd have rented a convertible.

Imagining the ride with the top down and wind blowing my hair, I let my fingers press the buttons to roll down both front windows of my smelly rental. I tilted my head toward the driver's side open window, squinting my eyes against the incoming wind. It felt good and even smelled good, like a vacation.

To my right were rows and rows of subdivision homes and just ahead, bigger buildings began to appear on the beach as Ocean Shore Boulevard made a gradual curve away from the shoreline.

Though only small dots in the distance, the sheer numbers of people on the beach was staggering. It was evident that I was approaching the place to be. A quick glance at my phone showed I was only a half mile or less from Antonio's address.

I slowed the car and guided the steering wheel as the road began its curve inland between the first two large resorts. The subdivisions on my right had disappeared and taking their place was a mix of hotels, restaurants, and bars. Brightly colored umbrellas shaded the many patio tables set up outside of the buildings in the open air. My eyes gleamed as I scanned back and forth observing the countless small crowds and groups of people who walked along the street, waited at the crosswalks, or relaxed around the patio tables sipping cocktails.

I pulled into the parking lot of some hotel on the left, found an empty space, and stuffed my backpack on the rear floorboard behind me. The crowded beach was visible beyond the hotel via a wide, paved pathway lined with colorful flowering plants on each side.

I wasn't ready for Antonio at that moment. I needed a short break and something to eat. A distraction, even if only a temporary one. A few moments of calm would get my emotions in check because, I knew, things would begin to unfold shortly. I had to prepare myself for a possibly tense escape and quick drive north. Daytona Beach was not the ideal location for any type of confrontation. There were eyes and ears all around and the busy two-lane highway with only two main directions of ingress and egress made me nervous.

Walking out onto the beach, I pulled up Antonio's address again on my phone. I changed the mode to satellite view and zoomed in.

In front of me, hundreds of bronze-tanned bodies stood out as a sharp contrast to the white sands. To the right, a beach volleyball game was going on, creating its own spectator grouping. And to my left, a line had formed snaking its way to what looked like a little tiki bar or concession stand. Over everyone's heads, all I could see from where I stood was a wood-shingled roof with a large replica of one of those martini paper umbrellas mounted above the roofline.

Falling into line behind some big guy wearing a red speedo, I focused on the aerial map view of Antonio's house again. His was a large lot. In fact, the largest single lot anywhere nearby. It was on the beach side of Ocean Shore Boulevard. A priceless piece of real estate. The aerial view showed an expansive white roof of the structure centered in the lot surrounded by trees and bushes. There was a pier that went right out onto the sand and a swimming pool near the home. The pool appeared to be slightly toward the southern end of the home. The beach was to the east and Ocean Shore Boulevard to the west. Antonio's home was sandwiched between the busy beachfront and the never-ending traffic of the road and that fact affected me, draining some of my optimism for an easy exit.

It appeared that the only area void of vegetation on the lot was between the home and the beach. It made sense. If one can afford a beachfront home, then they'd surely want the beachfront view.

In my distraction, I wasn't paying attention to my line and I felt a tap on my shoulder followed by a, "Hey, move up, please."

I stepped forward and went back to my phone screen. I could park somewhere near the home unnoticed and enter his property through the north and chance being seen by any neighbors. Or, walk along the beach until reaching the edge of his land where the trees began. Either way, simply walking into the house and announcing myself as the lady he tried to kill probably would not be the best of ideas.

I tucked the phone into my pocket as the line neared the tiki bar with only three people left to order in front of me.

Not quite dressed for the beach, I was beginning to feel a bit overcooked from the sun's rays heating up my black clothing. Droplets of sweat rolled down my spine, coming to rest at the spot where the leather holster for my thirty-eight touched the small of my back. It itched, but I dared not reach back to scratch, as the outline of the hidden weapon through my shirt would be easily picked out by anyone with a clever eye.

"Next," a girl inside the tiki bar said loudly. The bar wasn't nearly as unique as I'd expected. It was actually a small cargo trailer dressed up with wood siding, a roof, and two dropdown windows. The trailer hitch stuck out toward the beach with a big orange cone in front of it for safety.

I moved around the guy in the red speedo to the next window over and stood at the wooden counter made from a piece of plywood that was held up by chains on each side of it. A chalkboard menu hung between the two windows.

The girl leaned toward me with her elbows on the counter, waiting patiently.

"I'll take a Coke, hot dog, and a pack of those," I said, pointing to the cigarette rack on the back wall of the tiki trailer.

She reached back to where I pointed, "These?" she asked.

"No, next over," I said.

She pulled the pack from the rack and held them up in a questioning manner.

I nodded, said, "Yep, those," and handed over my credit card.

Taking my meal and cigarettes, I found a shaded plot of beach near the volleyball game and sat down on the warm sand by two mothers whose eyes were fixed on three kids out near the water's edge beyond the volleyball net. Sitting there picking at the hot dog with the Coke shoved in the sand at my side, I observed the activities around me. So many people. So much going on. It was both a blessing and a curse.

Taking a sip of my drink, I realized at that moment that I'd need to fit in better.

Turning to the two mothers, I said, "Excuse me." Once I was acknowledged, I asked, "Is there anywhere around here that sells swimsuits?"

One perked up, "Oh yeah, on the other side of the road back there," she said, pointing to Ocean Shore, but more north of where I'd parked. "It's a little shop. Not much selection, but it's the closest place I know of."

"Thank you, ladies," I replied as their focus returned to the kids.

"What color swimsuits do you sell the most of?" I asked the guy in the little clothing shop. He was all Florida, wearing short shorts and a bright neon green tank top. It appeared the mother was right, there was not a huge selection.

Without hesitation, he replied in a drawn-out feminine tone, "Reds and blues this year. I'd say red, though. The lifeguard look seems to be in style. You want a one-piece or two?"

Normal me. The old me. The mother of twin girls me would have said a one-piece. But not only did I need to blend in, I needed to impress and distract, if only for a few short seconds. "Two piece … one with minimal coverage."

He smiled and looked me up and down. "You out here on the hunt, I see. Gonna find you a man."

I bit my lip and winked. "I am. Yes, I am."

"Girl, I got just the one for you," he said, grabbing a bright red bikini from the top rack. "This is the one. This one will tell them men, 'hmm honey, come and get me'." The strings dangled loosely as he handed me the hanger. "You can try it on. Dressing room is around the corner."

Inside the dressing room, it was hard to strip down from what I had become so used to wearing lately. The black t-shirt and cargos had not only turned into my own personal identity, just like the goth clothes and make-up of my childhood, the appearance was a wall that I could hide behind again. The style had become all too comfortable, physically and emotionally.

Piling all my clothing onto a chair in the corner of the small room, I slipped on the bikini bottom, pulling it up tight. It fit. It fit good. I turned around to view my backside. When I looked over my shoulder, the first thing that caught my eye was the two scars. The entrance and exit wounds from Aspen.

Blocking any thoughts of them from my mind, I let my eyes move down to the tight red bottom, I was impressed. The side strings rode high up on my hips, making the edge of the fabric cut across my butt cheeks in the perfect way. I'd have to save this for Daniel.

I rose to my tip-toes and with both hands, ran my fingers between my skin and the bikini fabric from my hips down, tugging the red sexy triangle into place.

After tying on the top, I spun around to see myself as I hadn't in many years. I didn't quite fill in the top, but nothing could be done about that. Still though, I looked damn good. The fact that I had not been eating well might have helped. Actually, the lack of decent food helped my look a lot, though probably not doing much for my health. Rubbing my hands up and down my torso, I liked the way it felt. My body was ... tight again. Not so much muscle, but tight. No loose areas.

Perfect.

The shop guy's jaw dropped in a dramatic gesture when I walked out of the dressing room in only the bikini and my tennis shoes. Cradled under my arm were my t-shirt and cargos.

"Oh, you are smokin' girl," the shop guy said loudly with a sway of his head and flip of his wrist. "Smokin'."

"Thank you," I replied with a sincere smile.

He continued, "Mmm mmm, that look is you. I was right. The red with that black hair. You are ... you are a fox."

My mind returned to my task and I said, "I need two more things."

"What's that girl?"

"A big shoulder bag and a pair of sunglasses."

Strutting past me to a basket near the door, he dug out a red and white striped shoulder bag made of some sort of wicker or straw. He tossed it to me and buzzed to the furthest corner of the store. There, up high, was a hanging display with various sunglasses. He peered over his shoulder at me, studying me, then flipped his head back and pulled down a set of silver-rimmed aviator glasses with mirror tint.

The guy was something else. His mannerisms and his quick movements were addicting. Not because of the uniqueness of him, but because he was so happy. I couldn't help but smile.

With a sashay in his walk, he came directly to me with the sunglasses aimed at my face, fingers of each hand grasping the temple arms of the frames. Upon reaching me, he glided the sunglasses smoothly onto my face, stood back and rubbed his chin with one hand. His head cocked to the side. "Yes, I like," he said and pointed to a mirror on the wall.

Facing the mirror, I too liked what I saw. Sure, the glasses complemented my black hair nicely, and the red bikini had me looking like a Florida native, but what I liked most was that the reflection bore no resemblance to Kaitlyn Cline, an attorney in her mid-thirties.

I dug out my credit card and handed it to him. "It's perfect. I'll take all of this."

chapter forty-six

At the rental car, I kicked off my tennis shoes and threw them on the driver's side floorboard, slid into the seat, and chunked my t-shirt and cargos along with the undergarments into the passenger seat.

Reaching onto the rear floorboard, I retrieved my backpack and set it in my lap. I looked all around me to make sure there were no prying eyes, then unzipped it, removing the nine-mil with its silencer still attached and carefully laid it inside my cute new beach bag along with the pack of cigarettes I'd bought earlier.

I sat up to see my reflection in the rearview mirror, straightened some stray hairs that were caught up in the sunglasses and licked my lips. I had no lipstick, but the moisture made the dryness go away, giving my lips a sexy shine. It was more of a show of confidence to myself, as I was keenly aware that I'd be very much out of my comfort zone as soon as I stepped out of the car.

I was barefoot and wearing nearly nothing. If I had to make a run for it — well, I tried not to think of the negative.

Climbing out of the car in only the red bikini and sunglasses with the bag over my shoulder, I shut the driver's door and smirked at my reflection in the window.

I'd made a point to leave my wallet and phone in the console. The gloves. It was a gamble leaving them behind and I knew it. Wearing gloves would be a dead give-away and besides, I really doubted anyone would be dusting for fingerprints after today.

I immediately blended in when I went out onto the beach. It felt a little weird because I'd never *tried* to look like everyone else before. Standing out had always been my goal.

Strolling south along the beachfront, not a single person noticed me. The anonymity was interesting. I was … I was invisible.

From studying my phone earlier, I knew exactly which home I was looking for. It would be the only one with a large yard and trees. The roof was white and the pool would be located to the southern side of the yard. What I didn't know was how the home was set up, where the doors were, alarms — cameras. And if Antonio would even be there.

The beachfront estate was obvious as I continued in my southerly direction. The large trees stood out from a distance. With each few steps, more and more of the property revealed itself. A stand of trees flanked the entire north boundary, somewhat thinner than the aerial view led me to believe. However, the vegetation on the southern boundary contained thicker brush, fewer trees, and more cover.

Nearing that northern boundary, I could see the back of the house. Similar to Jeff's mansion, this one also had huge windows. Floor to ceiling, spanning the entire length of the rear. The main difference was that this home was only one level. One massive, spread out level.

Passing directly behind the home, my phone image was correct, there was nothing blocking his ocean view. No trees, no fence, nothing.

After closing in on the southernmost boundary of the property and not so much directly behind the home, I stopped a few feet away from a rather widely-dispersed group of about eight people. Not close enough to make them uncomfortable, but close enough that the average viewer would think we were all together. Mine made the third red bikini in the mix and one other woman had a bag over shoulder just as I did.

I stood perpendicular to the estate, facing south along the beach. But using the sunglasses as cover, my eyes were intently focused toward Antonio's home. The entire back of the home was one long sitting room lined with windows. To the north end of the home, the most right from where I stood, a door was cracked open, likely to let the ocean breeze in. Everything inside was either white or of a similar light hue. Thankfully, the windows did have shades. I noticed two of them were pulled down. The rest were up.

A seating section was set up near the center of the room. It consisted of a couch facing the beach, one other chair perpendicular to the couch and a coffee table with a wooden top. In the middle of the coffee table was what appeared to be a small box. To the extreme right was a kitchenette with a bar with three stools lined up, covered in a white fabric, of course.

Shifting in the sand, I faced the ocean again. Luckily, my group of people still chatted away about which club would be best for an evening recap.

I twisted back in the sand facing the group again, once more peering sideways through the glasses to the home. Under the eaves on each distant corner, I could see cylindrical objects hanging, one on each side. Cameras. Aimed to the center of the back yard. Criss-crossing each other to provide the most security coverage.

Movement.

A figure entered the room from an interior door at the back left corner of the room. I spun toward the ocean, ran my fingers through my hair and let my head scan the horizon in order to appear as normal as the rest of the group.

I let my gaze slowly return to the home and saw the figure standing near the cracked-open door. It was him. He had on a white suit similar to the one he was wearing in New Jersey. Even if I were to ignore the suit choice, his silver hair, dark skin, and posture gave him away. It was him. That was the Antonio Fuentes I watched with Jeff. Backing away from the door, he returned to the interior door and made his exit from the room.

With the room empty again, my nerves returned almost to a normal state.

Taking in my last view of the blue waters, I headed south just behind those who were still going over their plans for the night. As soon as I passed the edge of Antonio's property, I doubled back behind the cover of the thick brush. Behind the brush, I could only see the very top of the white roof. Working my way further inside it, my feet tightened at the tiny stabs from the sticks and leaves.

I was not accustomed to being barefoot.

Branches reached out to scratch and prick at me as I squeezed into the denser interior of Antonio's tiny forest. Finally encapsulated in the thick greenery, neither the beach nor any of its patrons were visible.

To the front of me, I could only make out patches of white from the home's siding. I craned my neck around, peering through the tight web of leaves until I found the southern corner. And the hanging camera pointed to the yard.

Setting my beach bag down at my feet in the dead leaves, I pulled out the nine-mil, tugged the hammer back and aimed between the countless branches. My aim was at the nearest camera. Both hands gripped the pistol snug. Not too tight. Not too loose.

With nothing to steady my hands against, I closed my eyes for a moment, taking in a deep breath. Then, beginning to exhale, I opened my eyes and when the very last bit of air left my mouth, I applied pressure to the trigger with my index finger. The pistol jumped in my hand and I saw the camera quickly dislocate from its mount and begin swinging from an electrical cord.

I kept my position and waited for someone to come out to inspect as I began to count in my head.

By the count of thirty, no one had come out to investigate. Next. Using the long silencer to separate more greenery, I acquired a visual of the opposing camera.

Another eighty or ninety feet. That was the distance I'd guessed it to be further than my last shot. Adjusting my aim to account for the added yardage, I followed the same routine and made the shot. My heart stopped for that split second until I saw the camera flip out of its mount and begin its own deadman's swing.

chapter forty-seven

With the cameras taken out and no indication that their absence had been noticed, I returned to my spot on the sand in front of the estate. I was alone. The group that I'd used as my cover earlier had moved on.

The room was empty. Antonio had not come back. I could only assume that he was still on the premises since the door was still partially open.

Behind me and closer to the beach, some scattered tanned bodies were hanging around. Though not in close proximity, they were still within easy sight of the room. Unfortunately for me, there was the chance that their wandering eyes may see what was going to take place inside the glassed-in room of Antonio's.

I replayed Dad's advice in my head, *slow down, think and plan ahead.*

Pushing the sunglasses higher on the bridge of my nose, I stuffed my right hand inside the beach bag hanging from my shoulder. My fingers rested on the hard grip of the nine-mil inside. My thumb casually brushed the hammer.

In a hurried motion, my approach began. I marched right down the center of the wooden walkway and past the pool toward Antonio's home. Once on the concrete patio, I turned to the open door and entered the room, slamming the door shut behind me. Immediately, I began rattling on loudly. "Hey, Jamison, I'm here. Let's —"

As I blabbed on with my pointless words, my right hand remained inside the bag. I went to each of the three windows that were in front of the couch and dropped the blinds, providing me a visual barrier to the outside. "Let's get some alcohol and get liquored up. Jamison, are you here?"

I was facing the beach and nearly done tugging on the third window shade when the interior door burst open.

Instinctively, my head turned to see Antonio storm into the room and stand inside the doorway. "What in the hell? Who are you?"

"Oh hi, I'm here to meet Jamison. You must be the help, I guess. Can you tell him I'm here?"

Antonio's face turned red. "Who the fuck are you?"

"Yeah, I forgot. I'm Marly. Can you tell him I'm here, please? I really like that suit you have on, mister."

"You have the wrong house, little girl. Get out. Now."

Having finished with the blinds, I faced him, staring at him through the mirrored sunglasses. He was still pissed, but I saw his guard drop and eyes take in the bikinied body in front of him. "Little lady," he said in a much softer tone. "This isn't Jamison's house, this is my house." He reached behind him, swinging the interior door shut, then walked along the back wall toward the kitchenette.

I tipped my head to the side, smiling. "Well, I'm sorry, mister. I was sure this was his house. I'm really sorry. I'll …"

Antonio waved his hand and said, "It is ok, little lady. You took me by surprise. Let me offer you a drink as my sincere apologies. What would you like?"

I shifted my weight back and forth between one bare foot and the other to give off an air of naivety and told him that a water would be simply perfect.

His eyes were glued to me. "I'll have a Scotch if you don't mind. Go ahead and have a seat. Your water is coming."

Gliding over to the single chair, I took hold of it and dragged it in front of the windows, placing it right across from and facing the couch. The three windows with the drawn shades at my back. "I hope this is ok. I'm just so tired of seeing that bright sun. I need a break from it." Sitting down in the chair with my bag next to me and my hand still inside, I placed my feet on the edge of the coffee table thinking that if I'd planned this with more notice, I'd have painted my toenails.

Antonio wore a grin on his face as he came to me and handed me the bottle of water. It was ice cold and I felt confident enough in the situation to take my right hand from the bag to open the bottle and help myself to a drink.

Antonio did just as I'd hoped. He sat down on the couch across from me and took a sip from his glass while keeping his beady eyes on me. "Take off your glasses," he said. "Get comfy. Relax. Let us talk some. I find that meeting new people is very ... educational." The old man's hormones were beginning to flare.

I set the water bottle on the floor next to me and slowly removed the sunglasses, folded them, and with my right hand, placed them inside the beach bag. My hand remained inside the bag and my fingers returned to rest on the pistol. My bare feet still on the coffee table.

Antonio noticed nothing. He leaned back and crossed his legs. "Tell me your name again, señorita. I seem to have forgotten it in my earlier confusion."

I let my fake smile fade away as I looked him in the eye. "My name's Kaitlyn. Kaitlyn Cline. How are you, Antonio?" My hand tightened on the hidden nine millimeter.

His eyes squinted and his lips pressed together tightly as his brain registered my name and the fact that I knew his. The moment I saw his eyes widen and his body stiffen, I raised the nine-mil out of the bag, cocking the hammer in motion.

"You bitch," he shouted, uncrossing his legs and planting both feet upon the floor. "You are a crazy bitch! I will kill you!" The Scotch glass fell from his hand to the floor.

"Haven't you tried that already? You've failed. Now, I'm here to kill you."

He shouted again, "You bitch!"

The interior door burst open again. It was the guy with slicked-back dark hair and I recognized him instantly. Keeping my pistol aimed at Antonio's chest, I told him calmly, "Come, come. Sit down next dear old Antonio, please." I made a motion with the tip of the pistol. "Keep your hands clear now, handsome," I told him.

He held his hands out to his side and carefully walked between the couch and coffee table, then sat down, placing his open hands on his thighs.

"Scoot over some," I said.

He moved a few inches toward Antonio. He looked exactly like he did in my memory of that day.

"No, scoot over some more. Get close there to your boss." He did as I ordered. His leg touching Antonio's. Antonio was obviously uncomfortable with the seating arrangement.

"You don't recognize me, do you?" I asked.

His head shook and he replied, "No."

With a quick flick of my wrist, I directed the nine-mil to his chest and pulled the trigger. His body jumped and his mouth dropped open at the surprise. The life left his body as soon as he realized what had happened. His head and shoulders drooped to the side onto Antonio's white suit.

Antonio's expression of anger disappeared. His eyes became much less aggressive and he forced a smile onto his face. "Now Kaitlyn, we can come to an arrangement here," he said while at the same time using his shoulder to push his employee's dead body off of him. The lifeless corpse straightened upright before gradually falling onto the cushions away from him. A bright red streak of blood formed an arc against the back of the white couch.

Antonio was in a predicament that he was not used to. For one, being ordered to do anything must have been a memory he'd long ago forgotten. And secondly, I'm pretty sure he'd never had someone who he was wanting dead show up at his house. I held all the cards and he knew it.

He tried his best to regain composure saying, "Señora Cline, let us slow down for a moment. We can work this out. What do you want?"

"Nothing," I said.

"May I?" he asked, motioning to the small wooden box in the center of the coffee table. "May I have a smoke?"

"Sure. Go ahead," I replied, making a mental note of the gold ashtray near the box.

He tilted forward toward the coffee table, toward me. The proximity of him to my feet, still on the edge of the table, gave me jitters. But I didn't let on, or move my feet. His eyes never left mine as he opened the box and pulled out a cigar, then a cutter and lighter. Pointing to the open box, he asked, "You want? These are the best cigars money can buy. I promise. Let us share a smoke while we talk." His eyes parted from mine briefly in order to clip the end of the cigar and flip the top of the Zippo lighter, the same one I saw him use in New Jersey.

With my left hand, I dug into my bag and came out with the box of cigarettes I'd bought at the tiki bar. Flipping open the red and white lid, I said, "No thanks, I brought my own smokes."

He glared at the pack, watching me use only my left hand to remove one cigarette and close the lid. "Marlboro Reds," he said. "Ahh, an amigo of mine also smokes only those."

With no expression, I took my feet down from the table's edge and leaned forward toward him, way too close for my own personal comfort. I set the cigarette between my lips while he thumbed the lighter and held it to my Marlboro Red. I drew in a puff, sat back and said, "I know."

It may have been my imagination, but I saw what looked like a flicker in his eyes. He knew. He knew then that he would never get up from that couch again. His body language didn't want to admit it, but his eyes did.

His torso straightened and he inhaled deeply from his cigar.

I sat there with the nine-mil still serving as the mediator in the conversation, keeping things civil. Antonio exhaled a long trail of smoke and we both studied each other in silence through the white haze as it floated between us.

"Señora Cline, let me make you a wealthy woman. Right now. I write you a check. Then we can each go our own ways." He pointed to the left inside pocket of his coat. "May I? My checkbook is here, aqui."

With my left hand, I casually removed the cigarette from my lips, holding it between two fingers.

"Sure," I answered him with a nod.

I noticed a small bulge in the fabric of his coat.

The bulge of something of weight.

More weight than a checkbook.

I let him continue.

His fingers disappeared under the fabric slowly. His eyes on mine. His knuckles pushed the coat out as his he gripped it.

I let him.

He tensed. His thumb moved under the fabric.

I let him.

I watched him take in a deep breath. Then, in as quick as a motion as he could muster, he began the movement of yanking his hand out of the coat pocket.

My nine-mil was held barely above my thigh. My finger confidently on the trigger. Its aim corresponded with my eyes.

Time came to a halt.

The instant I saw silver, I let my index finger complete its cycle. The muzzle jerked upward. The flash came from the end of the silencer ... and a nickel-sized red indentation immediately appeared between Antonio's eyes.

All in slow motion, he seemed to keep his evil stare on me while his head twitched back forcefully upon the impact, sending his body to rest on the couch's cushion behind him. Splatters of red covered the back wall. A small stream of blood ran down from the entrance hole between his eyes, forming a narrow river that followed along the left side of his nose and down past his mouth where it dripped down, each droplet soaking into his white suit. The cigar still clutched between his fingers. A small and shiny silver derringer lay in his lap.

Letting the hammer down on my weapon, I placed the Marlboro Red back into my lips and stood up over the coffee table. I reached across and removed the cigar from Antonio's dead fingers. I extinguished it by twisting the lit end of it against the coffee table's surface, then set it in the ashtray. For my own smoke, I inhaled one more long drag and put it out in similar fashion.

I laid the remainder of my Marlboro Red alongside his cigar in the ashtray.

chapter forty-eight

Most events in life never match up to how we imagine them to be. They don't live up to the hype in our head.

My own homecoming did, though.

Somewhere between Florida and North Carolina, I stopped by a proper salon and had my hair fixed and colored back to my old and boring light brown shade. I'd picked up a white button-up blouse from a second-hand store and I had fabricated my story about how I made it to a remote cabin in the mountains after my accident in Aspen. My story included a concussion along with some short-term memory loss.

I told Daniel and the girls that I was helped by an older couple who were wanted for tax evasion. I said they were nice enough to nurse me back to health, but were hesitant to bring me into the city until I was well enough to travel on my own.

I hated lying to Daniel and the girls, but they bought it. They believed my wild story.

Daniel tearfully admitted that his heart had not given up on me, but his mind had. He told me his reasoning was based upon the time frame involved and so many articles he'd read about missing persons. He'd honestly come to the conclusion that I was dead. There was a lot of guilt over that, and I did my best to tell him those were thoughts anyone would have. My words didn't help much. Over the following few days, I made a point to hug him and the girls more and say those words that we all so often tend to skip over, "I love you."

No mention was ever made about my little note in the door. Daniel didn't ask about it, and I didn't bring it up, unsure of how I'd explain leaving a note and then coming back two days later.

He told me of the FBI agent, Scott, that had hounded him in the beginning and described to me how Scott and his team were following a strange trail of events that even included two dead bodies at a hotel.

I listened with interest and agreed with Daniel's opinion about how crazy it all sounded. Later that evening, I made a point to stuff all IDs and credit cards deep into some food scraps at the bottom of the trash.

Daniel had not given up hope, but my boss and coworkers had. A week after my return, I felt up to checking in for a meeting with our lead attorney, Brent McGillis. My plan was to talk with him about altering my assignments and hours so I could spend more time with my family. However, no words were needed. I noticed it as soon as I entered the firm. My office door glimmered brightly with its new name tag.

And ... I bought a used Toyota Camry, selling the Mercedes to an up-and-coming real estate agent. He informed me that he needed a more appropriate car for his *type of clientele*.

I told him I understood.

chapter forty-nine

It was a Friday night a few days later. The doorbell rang. I'd been making dinner with the girls. A simple task, but one I had dreamed of doing over my time away. Daniel went to the door, but didn't open it all the way. From the stove over the sound of searing vegetables, I could hear him talking. I couldn't make out any words, but from the tone and his body language, it wasn't a pleasant conversation.

Finally, he stepped aside, swinging the door completely open. A tall and young man in a navy blue suit entered, walking past Daniel.

The man's eyes were fixed on me as he walked in. The suit was cheap, but the haircut wasn't. His dark hair was nearly perfect, not a strand out of place. The way he walked through the living room told me that he'd been here before.

Daniel shut the door hard saying, "Kaitlyn, this is the FBI Agent I told you about, Scott Bertrand."

I wiped my hands on a towel and met the agent near the kitchen table. "Hi, Mr. Bertrand," I greeted with my hand out for a shake.

He shoved his hands inside the pockets of his slacks, leaving me there with my hand still held out. "Mrs. Cline," he said sternly with authority. "I am glad to see you back with your family and in such good health. May I chat with you for a few minutes?"

"Sure," I said, retrieving my hand from midair and crossing my arms.

Daniel made his way around the table, pulled out a chair and sat down. He rubbed his cheek as if he knew what was coming. Seeming all-to-familiar with this Mr. Bertrand fellow.

The agent twisted the chair across from Daniel to face me and sat down like it was his own home or office. "You can call me Scott. Please sit," he said, though it was more of an order.

The interrogation, as it was, commenced simply enough. I went through my story about the tax evaders, my memory loss, the cuts and bruises, and my eventual trip back home on a Greyhound bus. Daniel helped to fill in some of the other details of the story I'd forgotten, but I gave Agent Bertrand my solid and truthful account.

Unlike Daniel, the agent didn't buy it. Evident by his crossed arms and blank stare. His silence was tense.

Daniel huffed and said, "Scott, my wife has been through an ordeal. She's told you what happened. She's here now. She's alive. You can stop your investigation."

"Just tying up loose ends, Mr. Cline," said Scott. Directing his attention back to me, he asked, "If you had no ID and no credit card, how were you able to book a bus ticket?"

Thinking quick, I responded, "The ticket was paid for by the couple who helped me. I was never asked for an ID. I don't know why. Maybe the ticket person forgot. It was really busy there that day."

"That's odd," Scott said. "What day was that, Mrs. Cline?"

"What?"

Scott repeated, "What day was that?"

"I don't remember."

"Oh, ok. I thought you'd remember since you mentioned how busy it was." Scott stood up abruptly, pushed in his chair, and gave both Daniel and I a nod. "Thanks for your time. Good night."

I awoke early to sound of the girls goofing around in Olivia's room. Walking past her door, I thumped it with a knuckle.

"Yeah," one replied.

"Calm down in there and don't tear the house down."

Sitting at the kitchen table, Daniel was reading through the morning paper with a cup of coffee. "Hey, sleepy," he greeted, "I got coffee made."

I was barely awake and rubbing my eyes. "I can smell it. Thanks." I pulled a cup out of the cabinet and poured. "So, what's going on in the world?"

"Huh?"

"The paper. Anything important going on?" I asked. "You know, I've kinda been out of it lately."

He quickly sounded, "Hmm," closed the paper up and pushed it toward my seat. "Front page. Crazy stuff."

"Like what?"

"Drug dealers killing each other."

"Seriously?"

"Yeah, one drug boss in Florida got knocked off, so his guys went all the way to New Jersey to kill off the guy who did in their boss. Wild. Like in a book or something."

Those details struck a chord. I felt my stomach turn into a knot. "Wow, that does sound crazy." I added sugar and stirred it in, trying not to let my shaky hands tip my cup over.

"Come, read all about it," he said.

TY MICHAEL

Straight out of the wild, wild west.

In what investigators feel was a business deal gone bad for two of the largest suspected drug traffickers on the East Coast, a trail of blood that began in Daytona Beach, Florida ended in the small town of Montville, New Jersey.
 Sources say that Florida local, Antonio Fuentes, and one of his employees were assassinated in mafia-style fashion within Fuentes' beachfront home.
 Antonio Fuentes' remaining employees took matter into their own hands after determining that Jeffery Mitchell of New Jersey was to blame from clues found at the home.
 Days later, gunfire was reported in a quiet, upscale neighborhood in Montville, NJ. When authorities arrived, seven bodies were strewn throughout the estate. Inside, Jeffery Mitchell's body was found tied to a chair. His death was a result from a single gunshot wound.

Authorities are still trying to piece together the connection of these two men.

Citizens in Montville are in complete disbelief that Mitchell would have been involved in any unlawful activities.

In an interview, Mitchell's mother, Shirley Mitchell, who works at a local diner stated, "There is something wrong here. I raised up my boy good. He ran a good business. He'd never be involved with any of what they are saying." She ended by tearfully saying, "He was a good boy, a good man. He'd never. I just won't believe it."

I read the article and my heart sank for Shirley. I would've have never guessed. Sliding the paper to the middle of the table, I told Daniel, "That is crazy. Like the title says, the wild, wild west." I watched as Daniel took a sip of coffee. "I feel so sorry for the mother, Shirley."

"Why?" he asked sarcastically.

"She's so sweet."

Daniel squinted, "You said that like you know her."

"Obviously, I don't," I mumbled. "She just seems sweet. I feel for her."

My phone vibrated on the kitchen counter near the coffee pot where I'd left it. "Hold that thought," I said to Daniel.

"Yes," I answered. "This is Kait ... Kaitlyn."

"Mrs. Cline," a male-sounding professional voice said. "I am Doctor Drennan from San Juan Regional Medical Center in Farmington."

"Yes," I nearly whispered.

"I have some news. Are you in a safe place to talk?"

"Yes," I responded as I returned to my seat at the table. Daniel was staring right at me.

"I am calling in regards to your father, Erick Hildebrand."

I'd never known the name he had been using, so my brain had to adjust. "Yes, is he ok?" I knew better. Calls like this never come with good news.

"Mrs. Cline, are you able to come in to the hospital?"

My eyes began to tear up. "I'm in North Carolina. I can't get there immediately." I hesitated to ask again, but I had to. "Is my father ok?"

There was a silence of a few seconds, "Mrs. Cline, do you have someone with you now?"

"I do. My husband. Tell me ... please."

"Mrs. Cline," the doctor said, "I am terribly sorry to tell you this, but your father has passed away today."

I couldn't hold back the tears and I covered my mouth with my hand in an effort to hold back the sobs. Daniel stepped around and put his hands on my shoulders.

"Mrs. Cline, are you still there?" asked the doctor.

I could hardly speak. "Yes, I'll be there as soon as I can."

My trembling thumb pressed the disconnect button and I laid my head down on the table.

Made in the USA
Columbia, SC
04 July 2021